the serious kiss

the serious kiss

mary hogan

HARPERCOLLINS*PUBLISHERS*

The Serious Kiss

Copyright © 2005 by Mary Hogan

www.harperteen.com

Library of Congress Cataloging-in-Publication Data

Hogan, Mary.

    The serious kiss / Mary Hogan.— 1st ed.

        p.   cm.

    Summary: Relates the angst-ridden life of fourteen-year-old
Libby Madrigal as she tries to deal with her unhappily married
alcoholic father and overeating mother, moving to a new town,
and finding the perfect boy to "seriously" kiss.

    ISBN 0-06-072206-1

    ISBN 0-06-072207-X (lib bdg.)

    [1. Family problems—Fiction. 2. Moving, Household—
Fiction. 3. Alcoholism—Fiction.

4. Barstow (Calif.)—Fiction.] I. Title.

PZ7.H68312Se 2004   2004009612

[Fic]—dc22   CIP

                                                  AC

Typography by Sasha Illingworth

1 2 3 4 5 6 7 8 9 10

❖

First Edition

For Bob Hogan,
who makes it possible for
me to do what I love

acknowledgements

First, thank you Mom and Dad for being nothing
like the parents in this story! My deepest gratitude also
goes to the seriously talented people who helped create
this book: my brilliant and funny editor, Amanda Maciel, the
agent of any writer's dreams, Laura Langlie, and Deborah Jacobs
from the Scripps McDonald Center for Alcoholism and
Drug Addiction. Love and endless thanks to my early readers and
tireless support system: Bill Persky, Joanna Patton, Linda Konner,
Jud and Julie Hogan, Carol Gorman, and Robert Hogan.

the serious kiss

part one
chatsworth

chapter one

My dad drinks too much and my mom eats too much, which pretty much sums up why I am the way I am: a knotted mass of anxiety, a walking cold sweat. Three weeks ago, when I entered my fourteenth year of existence, I realized the only stable, solid truth in my universe: Being me isn't easy.

"Dinneroo!" Mom yelled down the hall like she always yells down the hall each night as she comes home from work. Her perfume instantly gave me a headache. The slamming of the front door and the jingle of her car keys woke Juan Dog. *Yip. Yip.*

"In a sec!" I yelled back, but I didn't move a muscle. Dinner scares me. In fact, *all* meals and most salty snacks freak me out. They trigger an inner horror movie: *Attack of the Killer Fat Cells.* It's not that I hate food. I *love* it. What's better than hot bread slathered in melted butter? Or Doritos with an extra blast of nacho flavor? My mouth is watering just thinking of it. But, given my genetics—Mom's size has never even come close to my age and Dad wouldn't need *any* padding to play Santa Claus—I realize that letting my guard down, even once, is an invitation for my fat cells to puff out like blowfish. I'm definitely *pre*-fat. And food is simply too hard to control, too easy to send your whole life careening out of control. So, when Mom called me for dinner, I ignored my growling stomach, lifted the phone back to my ear, wiggled my shoulder blades into the comfy warm groove of my bed, and kept talking to my best friend, Nadine.

"So what'd *he* say? Then what'd *you* say? Uh-huh. Then what'd *he* say?"

Through my closed bedroom door I heard one of my brothers playing with his Game Boy. "Get him! Get him! Get him!" I smelled the Mickey D fries Mom had brought home.

"Dirk!" Mom yelled. "Dinnerooney!"

My eleven-year-old brother, Dirk, is three years younger than me, but light-years from maturity. He's not what you'd ever call a high achiever. He's forever stalling for time, saying "Huh?" scratching his nose, and slurping back the pool of drool that builds up behind his hanging lower lip. Juan Dog the Chihuahua is almost my age, which, in dog years, means he's like ninety-eight. Juan is what you'd call high-strung. He yaps so much he levitates his tiny, quivering body all the way off the floor.

"Dirk!" Mom shouted. "Shake your *fannywannydingo*!" Did I mention my mother adds cutesy suffixes to words? She thinks it's youthful and snappy. I happen to know it's too embarrassing for words. One time, about a month ago, she called Juan Dog's business a *poopadilly.* Outside—in front of everybody.

Mom pounded on my bedroom door. "You still on that thing?" Like she hadn't clicked in on the extension twice already.

"Dinner's on the table."

"I'll be off in a minute!" I said. Then to Nadine: "So what'd he say?"

"Rif!" Mom screeched. "Where the heck is Rif?"

That was a no-brainer. Rif, my sixteen-year-old brother, is never around. He hides cigarettes in the tight curls of his ash-blond hair. When no one is in smelling distance, he lights up, takes a long slow drag, then smothers the end with two spit-wet fingers and tucks the cigarette back into his hair.

"Who needs a nicotine patch?" he says. "I got my own method." Whatever that means. One time, about a year ago, the right side of Rif's head started smoldering when he sat in the family room watching MTV. Mom was like, "Call the fire department!" Dad was like, "Isn't there a football game on?" My parents have never seemed like they belong together. And I've never, ever felt like I belong in this family.

"*Now*, Elizabeth," Mom pounded my door one last time. I groaned.

"I gotta go, Nadine," I said into the phone. "E-mail me later?"

"Yeah. Later."

I hung up, fluffed my flattened hair, and walked down the hall to the kitchen. Rif slithered in behind me smelling of burned hair gel.

"It's *Libby*, Mom," I said, rolling my eyes.

"Whatever," she said, rolling her eyes right back at me. Mom shoved a stray strand of her cottony overbleached hair back into the cat fight she calls a hairstyle. She tugged on her too-tight orange skirt, applied a new layer of magenta lipstick over the faded old one, removed black eyeliner goop from the corners of her green eyes, and tottered around the kitchen on spiked heels way too high for a woman of her age and heft. I'm not talking stare-at-you-in-the-mall quantities of fat, but my mother definitely hasn't seen her feet, or how sausage-like they look shoved into those strappy high heels, for quite a while. It's hard to believe I came out of this person. My hair is long and brown and shiny. My eyes are blue. I've never worn any makeup, unless you consider Vaseline lip gloss.

My brother Rif once graded my looks a "C."

"Who asked you?" I asked, visibly hurt.

"What's wrong with a 'C'?" he protested. "It's average!"

Which hurt even more. Who wants to be *average*? Mom stepped in for support.

"With a little makeover, honey, I'm sure I could turn you into a 'B.'"

Like I said, being me isn't easy. Isn't your own *mother* supposed to think you're an "A" even if you're not? While I'm at it, aren't your parents supposed to set a good example? I'm not saying that my mom and dad are *bad* influences—it's just that they haven't exactly set the family bar very high. I can't remember the last time I saw my mother pick up a book or my father put down the remote control. Mom's idea of the perfect family vacation is Las Vegas, primarily for the cheap all-you-can-eat buffets. Dad dreams of staying home alone with several six-packs while we all go somewhere that has no cell service. Once, he actually said to me, "You know what the worst thing about having kids is? They're always *there*."

Of course, I took it personally. Rif is *never* there and Dirk is still young enough to be ignored. I asked my dad, "Where do you expect me to go?" but he just shrugged and turned up the volume on the TV.

Mostly, it feels like my parents are the kids and we are left to raise ourselves. I mean, they provide food and shelter, but that's about it. Mom and Dad have too many problems of their own to bother with silly stuff like grades, parent-teacher conferences, nutrition, or helping me figure out the difference between maxi and *super* maxi pads and do I need wings?

The other night, as Dad and I watched the Discovery Channel's exploration of the nature-versus-nurture debate, I had a disturbing revelation. My inherited *nature* is filled with the potential for addictions, a butt the size of Texas, chronic self-absorption, word butchering, a fluorescent wardrobe, and truly hideous hair. As for nurturing, well, in my family "nurturing" is mostly edible. Last year, when I was upset that Nadine got into Honors English and I didn't, Mom baked me a tray of brownies and gave me a get well card. She signed it "Luv, Mom," which made me pretty sure she didn't get into Honors Spelling.

It became sickeningly clear that both nature and nurture were conspiring against me. What a rip-off! I have to overcome *Creation* if I want a normal life.

Beside me, on the couch, Dad burped, as if Creation were in total agreement.

I couldn't wait for the program to end so I could launch a searing discussion about how my dad could become a better role model, but he was already snoring by the final credits, and his undershirt was jacked up revealing a very hairy belly button. Somehow I knew, even if he were awake, he'd snore through my discussion and it would be about as successful as the hundreds of times my mom asked him to stop guzzling beer.

That night, I was forced to face the upsetting fact of my fourteen-year-old life: I'm on my own. It's up to me to create the life I want. I can't leave it up to chance any more than I can eat two slices of Domino's Pepperoni Feast pizza and *hope* my body doesn't notice the five hundred and thirty-four calories and fifty-six grams of carbs. I must be mistress of my destiny or I'll never even skim the surface of normal. I'll never have a boyfriend or a cool job or a passport with exotic stamps in it. Most of all, I'll never experience the one thing I want most: True love.

I knew exactly what I had to do. And that's when the whole fiasco began.

It was originally Nadine's idea. Maybe it was mine. We're like that, the two of us. Our brains are the right and left hemispheres of one consciousness. She's confident; I fake it. But I can't tell you how many times we've hatched the exact same idea at the exact same time. So, really, it's hard to say who thought of it first. The Serious Kiss popped into existence somewhere in the air between our two heads, right at the beginning of our freshman year.

"You know what I want?" Nadine had asked. We were lying on two blow-up rafts in the center of my dirt-flat backyard, tanning our legs. We'd both turned fourteen at the end of the summer, and were evaluating our lives with the wisdom that comes with maturity.

It was the first Saturday after school started. Already I was feeling majorly inadequate. I mean, Carrie Taylor spent a *month* in Greece with her family on some boat (she called it a "yacht") and had the smoothest honey-brown tan I've ever seen. I heard she used olive oil instead of Coppertone, but my mom said, "No way, *daisyfay*," when I tried to sneak ours out of the kitchen.

My own best friend, Nadine, was looking amazing, too. She'd grown taller, slimmer, and blonder over the summer. We've been best friends since she was short, chubby, and bicycled around our neighborhood with a hacked-up haircut her mother created with the Flowbee she bought on eBay. Now, Nadine's long, straight, much-blonder-than-mine hair is professionally trimmed. When she runs, her hair gently sways side to side like a hula dancer. She's a really good soccer player, too, one of those "natural athlete" types. At school, Nadine wears cream-colored yoga pants and little tees and always looks effortlessly pulled together. When I attempt a similar outfit, I look as though I forgot to change out of my pajamas. There's no way you can fake being a "natural" athlete. I've tried. Nadine just laughs.

"Maybe you should stick to basic black," she says, grinning, "to reflect the angst of your soul."

Somehow, Nadine bypassed black angst, along with chin zits and buck teeth and other teen horrors. She's the kind of girl who radiates health and makes you smile just looking at her, like you *know* she's nice. Which she is.

Me, I'm forever trying to raise my body-point average past, well, average.

Now and then, I wonder if Nadine and I would be best friends if we hadn't been best friends since we were kids who lived two streets away from one another. Does our connection have more to do with geography than chemistry? All I know for sure is, I don't want to put it to the test.

"You want NASA to invent ice cream that makes you

weightless," I said to Nadine, letting humor camouflage my jealousy.

Nadine laughed. "Yeah, that, too." We both reached for our Crystal Light lemonades at the same time and sipped from bendable straws. "But you know what I *really* want?" I knew. Of course I knew. I sighed. "Me, too."

"Wouldn't it be nice?"

"So nice."

"What do you think it feels like?"

Leaning back on the rubber pillow of my raft, I tried to imagine it. The "it" we were both talking about, of course, was the *big* IT, the IT supreme: Love. I'd pictured true love before. It was full of color, light. Pink feathers and turquoise ribbons and gold-leaf swirls that flickered in the sun. And it was cool, too, a blanket of satin, air-conditioning that never gave out and wasn't too expensive to run all summer, even at night. Love was soft and smooth and beautiful. Nothing like our cruddy old beige stucco house in Chatsworth, California, that sat smack in the center of town like a steaming burrito in the hottest part of the hopelessly suburban San Fernando Valley. Nothing like this yard that had started out as prickly weeds and was now nothing but dry, dusty dirt.

"Why bother planting anything?" Dad had said. "We're the only ones who will see it."

Like we don't matter, and it's only important if other people see it.

No, love was nothing like that. Real love was alive and vivid and out there for everybody to see.

"I think love feels like coming home," I said, adding, "if you actually like where you live."

Nadine laughed again. She always laughed at stuff I said, which made me feel wonderful.

"I think love feels like . . . like . . ." Nadine paused, looked over at me, then we both said the exact same thing at the exact same time: "Love is a serious kiss."

"Yes!" I said. "A *real* kiss. Not some slobber session beneath the bleachers."

"Not some stupid lap-dance kiss in somebody's basement."

"Not a fake kiss just 'cause some guy wants you to hook up."

"No, not a liar's kiss."

"No way." I stretched out on my raft and said, "True love feels like a deep, soul-melting, passion-bloated kiss."

"A kiss so intense you faint afterward." Nadine sat up.

"And he revives you with another kiss."

"He lifts your neck with the palm of his hand and kisses you back to life."

"You open your eyes," I said, my eyes drifting shut, "and see him gazing at you with such devotion your heart stops beating."

"Because he is your heart," Nadine said softly.

"And your soul mate."

"And everything in between." We stopped, sipped more lemonade, felt the cool, sweet-and-sour liquid trickle down our throats.

"That's what I want," I told my best friend.

"Me, too," she said.

"That's my goal this year."

"Mine, too."

We both sighed.

Nadine and I had been kissed before. I mean, we weren't lip

9

virgins or anything. But neither kiss had made the earth move . . . or even wiggle. Bert Trout, aka "Fish Boy," kissed Nadine at a junior high football game. He just leaned over and planted one on her.

"It felt like kissing a pincushion," she reported. "His mustache—if you can call it that—was all prickly and painful." It didn't help matters that he missed her mouth entirely. Fish Boy kissed Nadine's upper lip and lower nose, and, truthfully, she couldn't wait for it to end.

My neighbor Greg Minsky kissed me once, but it was way too juicy and it grossed me out. He tried a little tongue action, but no way was I going to gulp Greg Minsky's spit, so I basically shoved his tongue back where it belonged. After that, I pretty much kept my chin down and didn't give him another opportunity. Though he still looks like he might try. Greg rollerblades up and down our street whenever I'm out front and always finds some reason to stop and chat. It's cool. I like him, just not *that* way. He's too skinny, and his butt is a flat inner tube. Unlike me, he eats all the time. But he once made the mistake of telling me that food went straight through his system several times a day. Yuck.

"Yeah, I want a *serious* kiss," I said to Nadine. "A major smooch session. A kiss that means real love. That's my ambition this year."

"Mine, too."

Sitting up, I held up my left hand, placed my right hand over my heart. Nadine did the same. I said, "By our fifteenth birthdays, we, Libby Madrigal and Nadine Tilson, will experience at least one totally real, sincere, meaningful, soulful, poetic, inspiring, knee-buckling, love-filled, journal-worthy, insomnia-producing, appetite-reducing, mind-blowing, life-changing, unforgettable, undeniable, serious kiss."

"Just one?" Nadine giggled.

"If executed properly, one is all we need."

"Deal?"

"Deal."

We shook hands, felt excited. The plan was set. All we needed were two amazing, soulful, serious, kissable boys. That, and the nerve to pull it off.

What made me think—given my black angst and glaring deficiencies in the nature/nurture department—it would be easy?

chapter two

My locker wouldn't open. It was one of those days. Fernando High is one of those high schools. Nothing works, not even the kids who go here. Nadine saw me banging the ancient metal door with the heel of my hand.

"Kicking works best on mine," she said. Before I could stop her, she hauled off and gave my locker a Jackie Chan right in the gut.

"Na*dine.*" I stamped my foot. "We're going to get in trouble."

"Yeah, like it's our fault their lockers don't work." Nadine kicked it again. The metal bang echoed like a gunshot.

"Let me try that." Out of nowhere this guy named Curtis appeared and practically jammed his entire foot through my locker door. *Bang!* The noise attracted an instant crowd and a line of students eager to kickbox. *Bang!* Curtis kicked it again. I sort of knew Curtis from junior high. He'd made a name for himself by refusing to join the basketball team even though he was over six feet tall. The school jocks treated him like he was a traitor. I overheard him say that team sports took too much time away from his band. I think he played guitar, because the fingernails on his right hand were really long.

Shriveling into the huddle of students, I helplessly watched the dents appear in my locker, praying my locker mate *didn't* appear. Nadine giggled all girly because everyone was gawking, and Curtis, all macho for the same reason, rammed his huge basketball-sized foot against the metal door a third time. Paint chips sprinkled to the cement floor like dandruff. Still, the locker didn't open.

"I don't really need my notebook," I said, my voice about as small and weak as a baby toe.

But Nadine and Curtis had gone too far to stop now. Egged on by the crowd ("Bash it in with the fire extinguisher!") they were both about to fling their whole bodies at my locker when a baritone voice boomed, "That's enough."

Instantly, kids scattered. I froze, frantically composing a plausible explanation for my parents as to why I was expelled in the first month of high school.

Nadine and Curtis tried to run with everyone else, but the principal, Mr. Horner, whom everyone called "Mr. Horny," clamped one paw on each of their shoulders and said, "Come with me." To me he asked, "Where's your class?"

I almost confessed to not having any class, to being an idiot who let her friend vandalize school property, to often feeling so . . . so . . . *compacted* or something I could explode or, other times, hearing my heart echo in my chest because I'm so empty inside. I nearly admitted to living with a constant vibrating dread humming through my body, which feels as though, at any moment, when I least expect it—like *now*—something awful will swoop down and ruin my already-precarious life. I'll wake up fat or my parents will divorce or my hair will fall out or I'll finally kiss the boy who melts my skin when he kisses me back and he'll wait till prom night to announce to the whole school it was one big joke. Or my best friend will be carted off to the principal's office because of my stupid locker. I almost blurted out how awful it is to feel so uncertain, so out of control—like running on ice or having a rotten hard-boiled egg fermenting in my gut—no solid footing, a constant pre-hurl. I nearly dropped to my knees and begged Mr. Horny for forgiveness when he repeated, "Where is your classroom, young lady?"

Oh.

"Building C," I stammered.

"Get on over there, then, before the tardy bell rings."

"But it was *my* locker," I said. "It was stuck."

"Did you kick it?"

"I hit it with my hand," I said. Nadine and Curtis both looked at me. "My fist, I mean. I banged it with my fist. Hard."

"Get to class." Mr. Horny turned and led Nadine and Curtis away. I could tell Nadine was mad because her nostrils were stuck in the way open position. Curtis seemed to let it slide. On the way to the principal's office, he low-fived a straggler who, like me, wasn't going to make it to class before the bell.

"See you at lunch, Nadine?" I called after her, but she either didn't hear me or didn't want to.

It was hard enough trying to follow the hieroglyphics of Geometry on the chalkboard, but without a textbook, it was nearly impossible. I mean, we were learning about quadrilaterals in the first month? What was *that* about?

"Share with Ostensia," Mr. Puente said after he found out my book was still stuck in my stuck locker.

"Uh . . ." Before I could protest, Ostensia was practically sitting on top of me, her desk glued to mine, her garlic breath all over my face. I liked her, had known her since sixth grade, but, man, those homemade concoctions she unwrapped all day at school were aromatic enough to scare vampires away.

"Right here," she pointed, "page twelve. Halfway down, right hand si—"

"Got it," I whispered, then resumed holding my breath.

Truth be told, dividing a quad into triangles didn't interest me in the slightest. And determining the diagonals of a rhombus thrilled me even less, especially when my best friend was in trouble because of me, my locker looked like a car wreck, and the only reason I'd taken Geometry in my freshman year was because Carrie Taylor's boyfriend, Zack Nash, took Geometry with Mr. Puente, and he was the boy I'd decided to kiss. Well, not *decided,* actually, unless you consider a pounding heart a decision.

Zack Nash is the boy that I love. There, I've said it. Whew! It has been said. No one knows. Not Nadine or my mom or even the diary I started over the summer that didn't make it past June. I've loved Zack Nash since I first saw him walk across the lawn of Mission Junior High last year holding Carrie Taylor's pinky in his fist. I'm quite sure Zack Nash doesn't even know my name. Still, I've dreamed of his hand reaching for my pinky and his lips calling me home with one velvet kiss.

"Want one?" Ostensia peeled opened a foil-wrapped plate of

congealed nachos under the desk. The smell rose up like a rotting mushroom cloud. I shook my head and turned away. My stomach let me know I couldn't look at it again. "Later, then," Ostensia whispered. "I have lots."

Out of the corner of my eye I saw Zack Nash wave his hand back and forth in front of his pinched face. He turned around to look at me, his cocoa-colored eyes staring into my love-struck baby blues. I felt a zap of electricity shoot down my arms. I grinned, tried to look petite. Then, he curled his lip and said, loud enough for the whole class to hear, "Who cut the cheese?"

Of course everybody exploded in laughter. "Settle down," Mr. Puente said, but even he smiled. Ostensia looked all innocent, and I blushed purple. My curse—to look guilty even when I'm not.

"Let's move on," Mr. Puente said.

I held my breath, hoping the blood would drain from my face faster.

"Libby? Would you like to come up to the board and draw a parallelogram?"

"Mr. Puente, would you like to kiss my . . ."

That's what I wanted to say. But of course I didn't. In fact, I even understood it was Mr. Puente's way of saving me from being mortified in front of Zack Nash and God and everybody. But come on! How would standing in front of the whole class *save* me from embarrassment? Hadn't Mr. Puente learned anything about teenage humiliation in his years of humiliating us? Not to mention the fact that Geometry had really messed with my head. I'd been a pretty good student before. It always took me about fifteen minutes to figure out what teachers expected of me, then another fifteen to produce it. I was great at that—becoming whatever anybody wanted me to be. But Geometry was my undoing. When I wasn't staring at the smooth creamy skin on Zack Nash's neck, I was gaping at the chalkboard without a clue. Geometry, for me, was how I imagined people who couldn't read saw the world: shapes and squiggles that made no sense whatsoever.

"Libby?"

I forced myself to breathe again.

"No, thank you, Mr. Puente," I stammered. Hey, I gave it a shot.

"Come on up here and we'll work it out together." Mr. Puente held a stubby piece of chalk in my direction.

Ostensia exhaled and said, "You can do it."

Refusing was useless. Mr. Puente could stand there for hours holding that piece of chalk. I'd seen it before. He never gave up. So I stood up. My chair scraped the linoleum floor. The class got really quiet. Tucking my hair behind my ear, I slyly glanced at him. Yeah, he was looking. Zack's head was tilted up and his lips were parted and his beautiful neck swivelled at the same speed I walked. My heart thumped overtime, my cheeks were still aflame, and a dewy coating of sweat veiled my forehead. I could hear my sneakers squeak across the floor. But that's all I heard of the external world. The rest of the noise was deep within my head: buzzing in my ears; blood squeezing through my clenched veins; quick, shallow breaths burning my chest.

"A parallelogram," Mr. Puente repeated, handing me the chalk. But I heard it as a deep echo: "Paraaaaaallllllellloooooo-graaaam."

Standing with my back to the class, arm raised to the board, chalk perched between my thumb and forefinger, I went numb with panic. I could feel tumbleweeds rolling through my empty skull, hear the dry prairie wind. Once, on late-night cable, I'd seen a psychic hold a pen in her hand over a blank sheet of paper and summon the spirit of James Joyce. I tried it.

"Einstein," I whispered under my breath. "Are you there?"

"What?"

I turned to face Mr. Puente. His eyebrows were raised. He asked again, "What did you say, Libby?"

What *could* I say? I was busted. Big-time. He might as well have asked me to draw a road map of Uzbekistan—I didn't have a clue. Sighing, I tossed the chalk onto the ledge beneath the chalkboard.

"I said I could stand here for the rest of my life and not only not know how to draw a parallelogram but eventually lose the ability to draw a straight line, too."

The class laughed. A good, we're-with-you kind of laugh. Mr. Puente chuckled, too. I straightened my shoulders.

"An alien apparently abducted my brain over the summer and sucked out my capacity to understand two-dimensional shapes," I quipped. My face returned to its natural color.

They laughed again. Harder. I felt their love wash over me, felt empowered, giddy, reckless. Facing the students, my people, I raised my arms in the air, closed my eyes and cried out, "If there's anybody out there who can help me understand the first thing about Geometry, I'll help them with any other subject on earth!"

The class roared. I beamed. Peering through my eyelids, I saw Ostensia raise her nacho-smeared hand. I clamped my eyes shut.

"Anybody! Anybody at all!"

"I'll help you."

It wasn't Ostensia. It was male. A boy's voice.

His voice.

"Math is easy," said Zack Nash. "I need help with English. Essays."

English? Essays? I love English! I almost made it into *Honors* English. I speak English! Essays are my life! I could not believe that Zack Nash would offer to tutor me in front of the entire class. But there he was, his luscious eyes looking at me without a trace of sarcasm, his blond hair deliciously disheveled.

"You have two takers, Libby," Mr. Puente said. "Pick one, then take your seat so we can get on with class."

Looking out over the bright, full-moon faces of my classmates, I saw Ostensia and Zack Nash, both staring at me, smiling hopefully.

I said, "Zack Nash, I guess. Why not?"

Ostensia's face fell. The walk back to our double desk was long and awkward. She wouldn't look at me. I felt awful. Hideous. Like one of those girls who dumps her friends in the dirt the moment a guy comes along.

It was the happiest day of my life.

chapter three

"Dirk, wash your hands for dinner." Mom reached her own hand into the KFC bucket, tore off a piece of Extra Crispy skin, and sucked it into her mouth. Junk food again. My mother had actually believed Ronald Reagan when he said ketchup was a vegetable.

"I did wash my hands," Dirk said.

"Wash them with soap. Rif, grab the ketchup in the fridgeroo."

"It's on the *table,* Mom."

Yip.

"Juan, get out from under my feet! Who fed the dog?"

"I did," I said. "Can't we *ever* have salad for dinner? Or something you don't order through an intercom?"

"Rif, feed the dog."

"I *fed* him, Mom!"

"Where's Dad?" Dirk, unwashed, was already seated at his place.

"He's on his way," said Mom. Then she sighed. My brothers

and I looked at each other. We heard that sigh a lot.

Dinner was yet another psychotic break with reality. Nobody listened to anybody else. Mom threw together a fast-food fat fest before Dad got home; Dad's homecoming made us all nervous wrecks. Would he be Jekyll or Hyde? Could we talk to him or would dinner be one tense swallow after another? Eating has never been a pleasurable experience in my house. Unless, of course, I sneak a bag of Pepperidge Farm Milano cookies into my room and eat them alone in bed. Then, it's heavenly, though I have to speed-walk nearly an hour just to burn off three of them.

Mom nervously bit into a biscuit. Mouth full, she mumbled, "Bethy, please pour the milk."

"It's *Libby*, Mom. *Libby!*"

"Oy." She sighed again. "Who can keep track?"

Mom had a point. I *was* into frequent name changes. Hey, was it *my* fault my parents gave me a name with so many variations? What—they expected me to lug "Elizabeth" around for life? Or worse, "Bethy"? I can't tell you how many times people said "Betsy?" each time I said my name. "No, it's *Bethy*," I'd respond. "As in Elizabeth, Beth, Bethy." "*Ah,*" they'd say back, then pretty much refuse to say my name at all after that. Who wants to *th*ound like they have a li*th*p? "Libby" was way more grown-up, anyway. Nadine had suggested it. Back when she wasn't mad, back when she was my lifelong best friend.

Often, I wished I could trade families with Nadine. Nadine's parents are nothing like my parents. Her family is a pasta sauce commercial. Everybody is always laughing, crammed into the kitchen, encircling a large steaming pot on the stove. Her mom dips a wooden spoon into the vat of spaghetti sauce for a taste, good-naturedly swats her husband away. He hugs her, nuzzles her neck. Her little brother tosses a football with his buddy on the backyard lawn, a golden retriever sweeps the floor with his tail as he eagerly waits for a morsel to drop to the floor. Nadine's older sister carries a giant salad bowl to the large real-wood table, shouts, "Supper in five minutes!" And they call dinner "supper," which is *so* cool.

My parents, on the other hand, are more like the embarrassing relatives. Get this: My dad's name is Lance, but the other salesmen at his work dubbed him "Sir Lancelot" as a joke. You know, the buffed-out knight of the Round Table (yeah right), the hunky guy who had a thing for Guinevere? But after they saw him snarf down a foot-long salami sub all by himself in less than five minutes and slobber beer down the front of his tie, they shortened it to "Lot." Which suits my dad perfectly because he's majorly into excess.

My mom's name is Dorothy, but she's always been known as Dot. So my parents are Lot and Dot. Couldn't you just throw up? People hear their names and assume they're this happy, chirpy couple. Mom wants to keep it that way.

"Nobody needs to know our business," she says all the time. Which really means nobody needs to know the *truth.* If our family had a motto—and of course we don't—it wouldn't be "One for all, all for one" or "Do onto others as you would have them do onto you." It would be "Don't tell anyone." We don't really live in our house on Bonita Drive as much as we hide there. Which probably explains why *Momaroo* has her own language. Shhh! Don't tell.

The last time I was invited to Nadine's house for "supper," I sat there and stared at everybody like they were animals in some exotic Family Love zoo. Their ease with one another takes my breath away. Whenever I'm there I try to memorize the way Nadine acts so I can act normal, too.

The front door opened just as I finished filling everyone's milk glass. Dad's rubber-soled shoes squeaked across the linoleum floor. Everybody got real quiet. No one knew if it was going to be a good night or a bad night. We held our collective breath. Except Juan Dog. *Yip. Yip.*

"Perfect timing," Mom said anxiously. "Dinner's on the table."

Yip. Yip. Yip.

"What are we having?" Dad asked from the front door.

"The Colonel."

"Chicken?"

"They had a special. I had a coupon." Mom tore off another chunk of Extra Crispy skin and devoured it.

"Haven't you heard about *hormones*?" Dad's voice was too loud, too slow.

I swallowed air, felt that rotten egg wobble around in my stomach for the second time that day.

"It's KFC," Mom said, swallowing. "Your favorite."

Yippety. Yip.

As soon as my father tottered into the kitchen, I saw that his glasses were hanging off the end of his nose. His mud-colored hair was sticking up on one side; his belly strained the buttons on his short-sleeved white shirt. My father's nose was several shades of red. As he got closer to the table, I smelled smoky aftershave and mouthwash-covered beer. That's when I knew for sure he'd stopped at a bar on his way home.

"Farmers feed chickens hormones so they have bigger breasts." He scowled. "You tryin' to turn us into *girls*?"

Mom didn't say anything. Dad asked testily, "Well, *are* you?"

"Of course not. It's KFC. They don't do that."

"Anything's possible," he muttered. When he was in one of his moods, he found fault with Halle Berry's navel. I mean, nothing was good enough.

"Honey, why don't you wash your hands and sit down at the table?" Mom said.

"I sell *swimming pools*, for God's sake. How dirty could I be?"

"Okay, then just sit down." She pulled out his chair. Dad landed heavily. Dirk's leg wiggled beneath the table. Rif sat stone-faced, and I crossed my arms and stared at the bubbles dancing atop my nonfat milk.

Yip. Yip.

"When a man comes home," Dad said, slowly enunciating each word, "he doesn't want *chemicals* for dinner. Understood?"

"Yes."

"A man does not want to be made into a *woman*."

Yip. Yippety. Yip.

"No, of course not."

Yip. Yip.

"A man—"

Yippy. Yip.

"SHUT UP, MUTT!"

We jumped. Juan Dog swallowed his final yip and slithered under my chair.

"Damn dog!" Dad shouted. Nobody moved while we braced for the hurricane. But Dad just sat there staring at his empty plate.

After a while Mom said, "Biscuit?" waving a red-and-white KFC box under my nose. The smell of steaming buttermilk biscuits was almost unbearably delicious.

"No, thanks," I said.

"Pass the biscuits to Daddy," she whispered to me.

Daddy?

Rif reached for the chicken bucket. "Want a breast?" he asked Dirk mischievously.

"Huh?" Dirk didn't get it. Mom glared at Rif as she shoveled mashed potatoes onto her plate. Then she handed the container to me.

"No thanks, Mom. Pass the coleslaw, please."

"Beans?" She stuck a plastic tub of barbecued baked beans in front of my face. My mouth drowning in saliva, I weakened. But the sight of my mother's chin glistening in chicken grease firmed my resolve.

"Thank you, *no*."

"Corn on the cob?"

I just glared. "Did you even *buy* coleslaw?"

Slack jawed, Mom looked around the table. "I thought I did."

Recrossing my arms defiantly, I announced, "There is no way I'm eating one thousand one hundred and ninety calories in one meal!"

"Eat *something*, Libby," Mom responded through gritted teeth.

Indignantly, I reached for the corn, though it might as well have been a biscuit with all the carbs. Is it too much to ask that my own mother follow our government's nutritional pyramid? Has she ever even seen a leafy green? Maintaining my own hybrid diet—low cal, low fat, low carb—was impossible in a house where the refrigerator's vegetable keeper had been removed to make room for beer.

Dirk reached across the table to grab the chicken bucket just as the doorbell rang. Mom's head jerked up. We all stopped and blinked. A visitor at our house at dinnertime meant only one thing.

Bill collector.

"Shhhh." Dad sent spit spray all over the table. "Nobody move."

Dirk's arm hovered midair. Rif stopped chewing. The doorbell rang again.

"He's not going to leave," Mom whispered.

We'd witnessed this scene before. The first time, about a month ago, Mom innocently got up and answered the door. From the dinner table, we heard her voice morph from a chirpy "Hello!" to a whispered "Leave the bill and I'll pay it tomorrow."

The second and third times, Dad answered the door and gruffly said, "We're in the middle of dinner. Come back tomorrow afternoon."

Of course, no one is home at our house in the afternoon, so this time, the fourth time, Dad tried a new approach.

"Pretend we're not here," he mouthed.

Dad scraped his chair back, wincing at the sound it made, and shakily stood up. He held his finger to his lips as he teetered on tiptoe to the window beside the front door. At the kitchen table, Rif mumbled, "Our cars are in the driveway. He knows we're here."

26

Mom glared at him. Dirk's arm, still extended across the table, started to shake. Rif whispered to him, "You move, you die."

"Eat," Mom commanded. *"Quietly."*

In slow motion, Dirk reached into the chicken bucket and pulled out a thigh, then he gently put it back and fished around for another piece.

"Touch every one of them, why don't you?" Rif snarled.

"Shhh!"

Dad tiptoed back into the kitchen and whispered, "He left."

"Then why are we whispering?" Rif whispered.

"Close call," Mom said, glancing at my father. He sat down hard and reached into the bucket for a piece of chicken.

Yip. Yip. Juan Dog started up again. Dad was just about to drop-kick him into the living room when he suddenly jumped.

"Holy sh—"

"Mr. Madrigal?" A man's face peered through the grubby Levolor blinds on the window over the kitchen sink.

"Get out of my backyard," Dad screeched.

This time Dad didn't have to tell us not to move. We turned into wide-eyed mannequins all on our own.

Yip. Yip.

"If we could just talk for a few minutes—"

"This is private property," Dad yelled. "I'll call the police."

Yipe. Yip. Yip.

"I have a right to be here, Mr. Madrigal. If I could just talk to you for a few minutes."

"I have nothing to say to you."

Yi–

"Shut up, Juan!" Dad's face looked like it was about to pop.

27

Juan shut up, but I could tell he was insulted. I mean, if a dog isn't supposed to bark when a stranger trespasses in his very own yard, when is he supposed to bark?

"We can work out a payment plan," said the head in the kitchen window.

Dad sighed. "We're in the middle of dinner." His tone softened.

Mom asked quietly, "Want me to go talk to him this time, Lot?"

Wiping his mouth with the back of his hand, Dad stood. "I'll take care of it," he said, suddenly sounding sober. Then, to the head, "Go back to the front door. I'll give you five minutes."

Dad tucked in his shirt, rubbed the blood and expression back into his face. "Don't stop eating," he commanded. Heads bowed, we ate. I heard my father walk through the family room and open the front door.

"Mr. Madrigal . . ." The male voice sounded tentative, scared.

Mom asked us loudly, "So, what did you kids do at school today?"

". . . overdue . . . final notice . . . foreclosure . . ." Scary words floated into the kitchen as we tried to swallow.

Mom sat superstraight. "Dirk?" she asked. "Anything interesting happen at school?"

Dirk nodded. "Mrs. McAllister asked me to read my essay on great white sharks aloud to the whole class," he said, grinning.

"The whole class?" Mom echoed. "My goodness." I could tell she was listening with only one ear.

". . . we want to work with you," the man was saying to my father. "We're not the enemy."

"Did you know that more people are killed by elephants than sharks?" Dirk asked.

"Is that so?" Mom crammed forkfuls of baked beans into her mouth.

"More people are even killed by dogs."

". . . can't leave without a check . . ."

"And a shark's teeth keep on growing back each time he loses one."

". . . I don't want to keep coming out here, either."

"Again and again, no matter how many times he bites something like a seal or a whale."

"Sharks don't bite whales," Rif said. "Any more corn on the cob, or is Libby going to eat all of it?"

I sneered at him. Man, the corn was good.

"They could, maybe," Dirk said, "if they could catch one."

"Whales are the largest mammals on earth, you idiot." Rif reached for a cob. No way was I going to hand one to him.

". . . that would be fine, Mr. Madrigal."

"Dot?"

Mom set her fork down, swallowed hard, and turned her head toward the front door. "Yes, dear?"

Dad asked, "Where's the checkbook?"

A shadow briefly covered Mom's face, but it vanished quickly. She said brightly, "It's in my purse. I'll get it."

Mom got up and left the kitchen table. Dirk said sullenly, "Sharks are pretty big, too, you know."

When my father returned to the dinner table, his mood had improved considerably. He rubbed his hands together, said, "Pass my favorite chicken." Mom handed him the bucket of KFC, but I noticed she didn't look at him. I'd seen that "not look" before. I knew exactly what it meant.

"Checks aren't *money*, Lot," she'd screamed at him one night. "There has to be money in the bank."

He hadn't listened then, and he wasn't paying any attention to her "not look" now. I felt sorry for my mom. It must be awful to live in such loud silence — so much to say with no one to listen.

"Is there any slaw?" Dad asked, flipping the pop-top on a fresh can of beer.

The first time I noticed my dad had a problem with alcohol, I was about ten or so. Before that, he was just my dad. I was his little girl. He made me laugh and feel special.

"Who's the be*thed* girl in the whole wide world?" he'd ask.

"Bethy!" I'd squeal.

For my eighth birthday, my father organized a swimming party at his office, on a Sunday, when they were closed. One of the perks of being a swimming pool salesman — your own backyard can be a dirt lot because there is a gorgeous outdoor pool at the office.

Mom tied helium balloons to the wrought iron fence around the pool; Dad made a sign for the parking lot that read PRIVATE PARTY. He also turned the office CD player up as high as it would go and pointed the speakers toward the pool. Images from that day are still clear in my mind — the thrill of having a party in a grown-up's space, so close to a busy boulevard, the hysteria of splashing girls in bright bathing suits, Mom's joy, Dad's pride. It was so normal.

"Your dad *works* here?" my friend Marjorie had asked, astounded. "Is he a lifeguard?"

"No, silly." I giggled in a superior way, feeling certain that my dad had the coolest job ever. "He sells swimming pools! If you want one, you have to buy it from him!"

I remember Marjorie's wide eyes. I remember Nadine's laughter, too, and playing Marco Polo in the pool, and seeing Dad playfully pat my mother's rear end and kiss Dirk on the top of his little head. That day, Rif was off with his own friends, and I was the *oldest* child, instead of the middle child. I ate cake in my bathing suit without even thinking about it. I invited friends over without worrying what they might see.

But that was a long time ago.

By the time I turned nine, fewer people wanted swimming pools. Dad stopped patting my mother's bottom and began measuring it.

"Is that your second piece of cake?" he asked her at my ninth birthday party in Chatsworth Park.

I remember the way she looked at him, her eyes wet. She didn't talk to him for the rest of the party, and I felt like crying even though it was my birthday.

Little by little, my funny, loving father faded away. His body was there, but *he* wasn't. Some other guy was living inside him. This stranger was sarcastic, unreasonable, short-tempered, and occasionally violent. He never hit us or my mother. Instead, he took his anger out on the walls. Behind several oddly-placed framed prints around the house, fist-sized holes gape. And the knuckles on my dad's right hand are bigger than they are on his left because they never get the chance to heal right.

"Happy fat day to you!" Dad sang to Mom that day in Chatsworth Park. Marjorie heard him. Her eyes went wide again.

This time, I saw fear and embarrassment in them. She knew something was wrong with my dad. And, worse, she acted like it was contagious. She went home early, and eventually she stopped wanting to play at my house. After a while, I stopped inviting anyone over. I didn't want them to see my dad passed out on the couch or smell his brutal breath when his mouth hung open. Nadine was the only friend who kept coming anyway. She saw what was going on, but we never talked about it. I didn't bring it up, and she didn't, either.

It took me a while to totally understand what was happening to my family. It wasn't until one night, four years ago, that I was absolutely sure.

Like I said, I was about ten years old. My parents were having a dinner party, the only one I ever remember them having. Mom had been cooking for hours. The house smelled all garlicky and yeasty like hot bread. Mom's cheeks were flushed and her voice was an octave higher than usual. She let us eat Wendy's hamburgers on trays in front of the TV.

"Clean up your own mess," she trilled. "Then go to your rooms and stay there."

Dad was dressed in one of his ironed white work shirts and pressed khaki pants. He wore loafers with little tassels. I remember watching those tassels bounce back and forth as he scuffed across the family room floor. I offered him one of my onion rings, he said, "No thanks," then plopped down in an easy chair and popped the top of a beer.

"Ah, Lot." Mom sighed when she saw him. Then she disappeared into the kitchen and we scampered off to our rooms.

Rif was sleeping over at his friend's house that night, but Dirk and I decided to eavesdrop on my parents' party through the heat vent in my room. It was easy enough to listen just by sitting in the hall, but lying on our bellies pressed up to the heat vent seemed more fun at the time.

". . . and he drove off and was gone for an hour and a *half*!" bellowed my dad's work friend who was one of the guests. (Dad was moonlighting as a car salesman then.) Everybody laughed. I heard Mom echo, "An hour and a *half*?"

"I thought I'd have to pay for that car out of my commissions for the rest of my life!"

They all laughed again. Then Dad said, "Yeah, like you'd ever make enough to buy that car." There were a few twitters, but the laughter noticeably dimmed.

Mom, her voice still unnaturally high, said, "More bruschetta, Sam?"

"Sure."

"More wine?" Dad asked.

"If you're pouring."

"He's *always* pouring," Mom chirped. I could tell it was a joke, but nobody laughed.

The dinner party got louder as the hour got later, and Dirk fell asleep on my bedroom floor. I left him there and lay down on my bed listening through my open door. Dad's voice changed entirely. It was louder than everybody else's, slower. And he said mean things.

"Never met a dessert you didn't like, right, Dot?"

I remember feeling queasy, ashamed for him. I was humiliated for my mom, too, because I heard someone say, "We really should get going," and my dad, all slurry, shouted, "Going? Was it something my wife said?"

After the guests left, which was shortly after that, my mom started to cry and my dad started to yell. "Just once, Lot," Mom sobbed. "You couldn't stay sober *once*?"

"It was a *party*! People *drink* at parties! I noticed that my drinking didn't disturb your appetite."

"If you could only hear yourself," Mom cried.

"If you could only *see* yourself or I should say, your*selves*."

That night, the word "alcoholic" first creeped into my head. I knew better than to say it out loud. I didn't want Dad's wrath aimed at me. I also didn't want to listen to my parents fight anymore. Even then, I knew there were some conversations a kid shouldn't overhear. Because once you hear it, how can you ever forget?

The next day, my parents pretended to be fine around us, but I knew. They wouldn't look at each other. Mom's jaw was set tight. Dad watched a lot of TV. After that night, I understood what I'd been witnessing for years. Alcohol stole my father from me. It replaced him with a man who was mean to my mother and made our whole family feel like hiding.

At first, I felt sad that my funny, loving daddy was gone. Then I got mad. He wasn't *kidnapped*; he took himself away each time he opened a can of beer. Why couldn't he bring himself back? And why did my mom let him go? Why didn't she make him go to rehab? How could a mother let her kids grow up with such bad role models? And who has only *dirt* in their backyard?!

When I wasn't angry at my father, I was terrified of becoming my mother. Without proper nurturing, wouldn't nature run rampant? Was it my destiny to endure whatever life dished out?

Just thinking about it made my mouth go dry.

"I'm sorry."

That's what I wrote on the subject line of my e-mail to Nadine that night after I finished my KFC corn-on-the-cob dinner. I'd tried to see her at school, but she stiffed me at lunch, and she had marching band practice after last period. I'd waited in front of the music room until some other band student told me they were practicing on the football field that day. No way was I walking clear across the campus to have Nadine snub me in front of the whole marching band and the entire football team, too.

"Please don't be mad at me, Nadine," I wrote. Then I stopped. As I sat in front of my computer, hands perched on the keys, I couldn't figure out what else to say. Yeah, I felt awful that my best friend was carted away because she was trying to help me. But did I tell her to kick the smithereens out of my locker? Didn't I say that I didn't need my notebook, and she kept kicking anyway? Doesn't anybody ever listen to me?

Suddenly I was furious. How dare she pummel my locker! And who let that jerk Curtis and his size thirteen feet mangle the door? Not me! What, she expected me to lie to Mr. Horny and say that I did it? O*stench*ia breathed her bad breath on me all during Geometry. Did she care? I spent the whole day without my books, I'm going to get an incomplete on my homework assign-ments, not to mention the fact that my locker mate was like *raving* mad when she couldn't get her lunch out of our locker. Did Nadine care? Did she? Plus, the greatest moment in my whole entire life happened that day and I didn't have anyone to tell! What, she thinks Zack Nash wants to be tutored by just *anyone*? What, she thinks it's no big deal that I'm finally ready to admit he's the boy of my dreams after a *year* of silently obsessing over him?

The phone rang. I ignored it. Let my brothers get it. My hands were flying across the computer keys. Exclamation points and boldface capital letters littered the text. It's about time my so-called best friend got a piece of my mind.

". . . time to take RESPONSIBILITY—"

"Libby. It's for you." Mom called from the family room.

I ignored her. Continued my rant.

"—for YOUR own actions!!!!"

"Libby! Phone!"

I signed it, "Elizabeth Madrigal, *true* friend." Then, I hit the Send button, yelled, "Okay" to my mom and reached across my bed for the extension.

"Hello?"

"Libby?"

It was Nadine.

"What do *you* want?"

"I'm in love!"

chapter four

Doesn't that just take the cake?

I know, I sound like an old lady, but doesn't it? Nadine ruins my locker, spends lunch period in detention with Big Foot Curtis, and ends up going to the movies with him Friday after school.

"He's so amazing," Nadine said to me the next day in the cafeteria, completely forgetting about our little tiff and not even mentioning my angry e-mail.

"Yeah, you told me."

"He plays acoustic guitar and bass. Can you believe it?"

"No. And I couldn't believe it when you told me on the phone last night."

"Mr. Horny made us sit in *total* silence for an *entire* hour, so we were *forced* to pass notes."

"Uh-huh."

"You cannot believe how well you can get to know someone without saying one single, solitary word."

"You want Pizza Hut or Taco Bell?" We were holding up the line. Fernando High's cafeteria was a miniature version of my own home. In fact, it could have been catered by my mom. Every year local fast-food hangouts bid for the privilege of delivering junk food to Chatsworth's future leaders. In an attempt to teach us democracy, the student body was allowed to vote. Apparently, my pencilled-in request for a salad bar was disregarded entirely.

"Who can eat?" Nadine squealed.

I picked up a chicken taco and diet soda and headed for the cashier. Nadine, twittering nonstop in my ear, made a humming-bird look relaxed.

"Two whole pages, front and back, of *stuff.* Amazing, real stuff. He's a poet, you know, not just a musician. I'm going to save those notes to show our kids."

Oh, brother.

"You know what the best part is?" she asked.

"He'll fix my locker?" That flew right over her head. Nadine bulldozed on.

"The best part is, if everything works out the way I think it will, the way I hope and *pray* it will, Curtis will turn out to be the boy who delivers the big one."

I swung my leg over the cafeteria bench and plopped down. Nadine sat beside me, facing out in case (yeah, you guessed it) Curtis walked by.

"You know," I said, "one hour of detention can't really tell you anything about a person." I was tempted to confess I'd spent over a year silently studying Zack Nash and barely knew him at all. But Nadine's mind was on her possibly very real love life, not my imaginary one.

"Sometimes one hour is all you need," she said softly, petting the back of my head in a superior know-it-all way that really frosted me.

"And sometimes it isn't," I shot back, yanking my head away.

Nadine just sighed. "You'll see, Libby Madrigal. Before the year's out, *way* before, Curtis and I will have a serious kiss. You'll see. I know in my heart it's going to happen. In my *heart.*"

I believed her, which was the worst part. It's not that we were in competition or anything. It's just that I wanted my serious kiss to be first. Or at least at the same time as hers. This way, I was just learning to walk, and she was about to win an Olympic gold medal in track-and-field. How had this happened? My best friend, my very best friend, had zoomed so far ahead of me she was a tiny speck on my horizon.

"Hey."

"Hey!" Nadine leaped to her feet.

Curtis and his friend Ray—or Roy, or some other one-syllable "R"—walked up to our table. Curtis asked me, "How's your locker?"

"Still concave," I said. Then, in response to Ray/Roy's dumbfounded look, I added, "As dented as it was yesterday."

Nadine said, "We heard that whole bank of lockers is going to be replaced."

We did?

"Curtis and I overheard Horny's secretary talking to the custodian over the phone yesterday."

Oh. *That* "we." Nadine and I weren't even a "we" anymore. I wanted everyone to leave so I could swallow my taco in one bite.

"At least Libby got her books out of there this morning,"

Nadine reported. Her voice wasn't usually so singsongy. I wanted to barf. "Horny had the custodian open it with a crowbar. They gave Libby and her locker mate a brand-new locker."

"On the far end of campus," I mumbled.

"Cool," Ray/Roy said. Then he wiped his nose with the back of his hand.

Curtis turned to Nadine. "A bunch of us are heading out to the Boulevard for a bite. Wanna come?"

"Yes! I mean, yeah, that would be great. I'm starving."

I just looked at her. Nostrils flared. The way she looked at me the day before when Mr. Horny hauled her off to the best detention of her life.

"Can Libby come, too?" she asked. Nice try, I thought.

"Yeah. Whatever." Curtis began to look impatient.

"You guys go ahead," I said, flipping my hair casually. "I'm tutoring Zack Nash and I have to find him anyway."

Nothing. Zippo. Not one word of recognition. Not, "Zack Nash? That cute guy?" Not, "Wow. I didn't know you knew Zack Nash." Nada. Zilch*arooney.* Nadine shrugged, spun on her heel, said, "Okay," and then left. Just like that. I watched her disappear across the school's front lawn. With Ray/Roy and Curtis, the boy she was going to seriously kiss.

Doesn't that just take the cake?

chapter five

Dad was trying to pop the neighbor's dog with a BB gun when I got home from school. He lay flat on his belly up against the chain-link fence in our dirt backyard, his face ruddy and his sweaty arms covered in earth.

"Mangy mutt!" I heard him scream.

My father's battle with Winnie, the white Maltese next door, was psychotic. He went nuts every time the dog barked, and the dog barked every time her owners weren't home. Obviously her owners weren't home right now. Apparently my dad *was* home, in the middle of a workday, which wasn't a comforting sign.

"Hold *still*, you wimpy floor mop!"

"Here we go again," Rif said, joining me at the sliding glass door. "Canine versus asinine."

Winnie is as neurotic as dogs can get. Not that I blame her with a gun-toting maniac next door. I swear my dad loves to hear the sound of our neighbor's car backing down their driveway. He gets very still, waiting. Then, the moment Winnie makes a peep, he's flying across the room to the closet where his old Daisy BB gun and extra box of BBs are stashed—off-limits to us, of course. A few weeks ago, Dad woke us all up in the middle of the night.

"Who took it?" he spat at us in a rage. "Was it you? You? You?"

Dad wasn't drunk. He was hungover, which was way worse.

"Nobody touched your BB gun, Lot," Mom said wearily, holding her robe closed at the neck. "The kids know better than that."

"I know better," Dad yelled. "I always put that gun on a tiny piece of paper so I'll know if someone used it. And that paper was on the floor."

"Maybe it blew down when we were in the closet getting something else," Mom suggested.

"And maybe Christmas will be in July this year," Dad snapped back at her.

Dirk tried to warm his bare feet on the back of his pajama legs. Rif stood stone-faced. I simply yawned and waited for Dad's steam to run out. I knew he didn't think I'd taken his stupid BB gun. I hated guns. It was me who tried to stop Dad from shooting Winnie until Dad threatened to plant a BB in *my* behind.

"Let's go to bed, Lot," Mom said.

"Not until I get a confession. Who took it? You? You? You?"

After each accusatory "you," my brothers and I shook our heads. For once I actually looked innocent, being too tired to blush or sweat. Finally Mom said, "That's enough, Lot. The kids have school tomorrow."

Dad cleared his throat, seemed to abruptly see the ridiculousness of his midnight interrogation. He's like that, my dad. His sanity occasionally catches up with his insanity and takes him by surprise. It's as if he suddenly remembers the way he used to be, before beer muddled his brain. At those moments, I can almost pretend things are the way they once were.

"Here she is," Dad would sing on Saturday mornings when I came to the breakfast table in my pajamas, "Miss Chats-a-worth!"

To be honest, glimpses of my old dad just upset me. When I'm sure he's lost for good, he shows up and gets me missing him again. I don't want to miss my father when he's right in front of me. Too many other things stress me out.

"All right," he said that night. "Go to bed. But we all know a BB gun is not a toy, right?"

"Right."

"It's a dangerous weapon."

"Dangerous weapon," we repeated in exhausted unison.

"That piece of paper must have blown down," he mumbled as we padded off to bed. Dirk said, "Good night" at the door of the bedroom he shared with Rif, then fell face first into bed. Rif excitedly whispered to me, "Now I know about the paper. Next time I can just put it back!"

So, that day after school, Rif and I stood in the family room watching the man who created us aim his precious air gun at a ten-pound ball of barking white fluff. The muzzle of the BB rifle poked through the fence. Winnie was hoarse from barking. Juan Dog, peering through the glass door with us, swallowed dry dog spit in terror.

"Who's top dog now!" Dad bellowed maniacally. Then we heard a pop and a loud *ping!* Dad never hit Winnie, which added to his frustration, but he often pinged the neighbor's swing set,

43

completely confounding the family who lived there. We'd see Mr. Halpern examining his pockmarked slide while scratching his head. Lucky for Winnie, Dad was a bad shot. Unlucky for us, he was a huge embarrassment (not to mention a horrible role model). How do you admire a parent who not only wages war with a little dog but always loses, too?

The worst was the time Winnie was in heat and Dad had shoved Juan Dog under a gap in the fence. "That'll mess with their heads," he'd snarled.

But Juan had just stood there, hunched up, shivering. Winnie's barking scared him. His ears drooped like two wet Kleenexes. He looked pathetically back at my dad, tried to shimmy backward under the fence into the safety of his own yard.

"What, are you, *gay?*" Dad had growled at him, blocking his reentry with the butt of his BB gun. It wasn't until my mom walked outside and shrieked, "Have you finally lost every last one of your brain cells?" that Dad abandoned his attempt at genetic sabotage.

With so much going on outside, I didn't notice what had happened inside. In fact, it wasn't until Mr. Halpern's car drove up and Dad scurried back into the house, that I noticed our living room couch was gone. That's also when I noticed my dad was still in his slippers.

"What happened to the sofa?" I asked.

"Nothing," Dad answered, then he peered out the window to watch Mr. Halpern examine his swing set. "Loser," he said, smirking.

Rif reached into his hair and left the room.

"Dad, the couch that used to be in the living room is gone.

Did you know that?"

"Of course I *know*," he scoffed. Then he asked, "What time does your mother usually get home?"

"In a couple of hours," I said.

"Good," said Dad, then he slapped his slippers over to the fridge, opened it, and pulled a six-pack out of the space where vegetables are supposed to be. I sighed. He said, "Not you, too, Libby. Not today."

I sighed again and went to my room.

My ears buzzed as I walked down the hall, past the gaping space in the living room, past Juan Dog who was cowering beneath an easy chair.

"Bethy is *meth*y." Dirk threw a used wadded-up Kleenex at me as I passed his open bedroom door.

"Dirk is a jerk," I replied, slamming my own door.

Inside, I lay down on my bed and stared up at the ceiling. It felt like I had a dictionary sitting on my chest. The Oxford English, unabridged. I took a deep breath, tried to relax, but my whole life felt like too-tight jeans. My own home was suffocating me.

How had I been born into this circus? How could I escape?

Reaching my hand up to my face, I felt the bump on the ridge of my nose, ran my fingertip across my straight teeth, traced my cheekbones. Picking up the ends of my long straight hair, I checked for split ends. Finally, I came to the conclusion I always came to eventually: I'd been adopted. No matter how many times my parents denied it, I just couldn't believe that the people I lived with were connected to me via blood and DNA.

* * *

45

The screaming woke me up. At first I didn't know where I was, but the smell of pepperoni pizza jolted my memory. It was dinnertime at the Madrigal house. Mom had just come home with our dinner on the passenger seat.

". . . just made the decision . . . without consulting . . ."

She was yelling at Dad.

". . . count on your support. Just *once* . . ."

Dad was yelling at her. They were both yelling right outside my bedroom door.

"Support?" Mom shouted. "Any other woman would have dumped you years ago!"

Dad shouted back, "I don't see anyone blocking the door!" To emphasize his point, Dad slammed his fist against my door.

Here we go again.

Heart pounding, my first reaction was to throw open my bedroom door, leap between my parents, and scream at the top of my lungs until they stopped screaming at each other. I'd done that before, *exploded* in front of them. Face purple, pulling out my hair, I'd shrieked, "Shut up! Shut up! Shut up!"

Amazingly, they had shut up. They'd stopped insulting each other long enough to tell me to go to my room. Which I did. Through my closed bedroom door, I heard them stomp down the hall.

"See what you've done to your daughter?" Mom had barked, not far enough away for me not to hear.

"Me? What about you? You're her mother!"

"And *you* are her drunken father."

After that, I learned to leave them alone. They had enough to fight about without fighting about *me*.

Like now, for instance.

"Bash up the whole house while you're at it!" my mother was screeching.

Dad sounded as though he were doing exactly that. So, I leaped up from my bed and wedged the back of my desk chair under the doorknob the way I'd seen them do on TV. No way was my raging lunatic of a father barging in to create an instant window in one of my walls.

Slapping on my headphones, I turned my CD player up high, trying to calm my thudding heart. Suddenly I remembered reading a magazine article about meditation. It said you could tune out the world by sitting still and breathing. Weren't you supposed to hum, too?

"This was *my* house and I'll bash it if I want to!" Dad's fist hit the wall again.

Was?

Cross-legged on my bed, eyes closed, I hummed. I tried not to hear the plaster chunks falling to the floor or Juan Dog's hysterical bark.

Humm. Hummm.

"Happy now?" Mom growled. "Maybe you broke your hand this time!"

Yip! Yip!

Hummm.

The phone rang, disrupting my quest for inner peace. I quickly untangled my legs, yanked off my headphones, and lunged for the extension in my room before either parent could get annoyed with the sound of the ring and yank the cord from the wall.

"Hello?"

"Libby?"

Bam! Dad hit the wall again.

Dirk shot out of his bedroom yelling, "Stop it! Stop it!"

Yip! Yip! Yip!

"Who is this?" I could barely hear the voice on the phone. All I wanted was to get rid of whomever it was so I could pull Dirk into my room and we could hum together.

"Dirk, get back in your room!" Then to my father, Mom sneered, "You think you're Mr. Tough Gu—!"

Bam! She screamed as Dad's fist hit the wall again.

"It's Zack. Zack Nash."

Yip! Yip!

"Lay a hand on me and you're dead. I swear it!" Mom shrieked.

"Zack?" My heart leaped into my ears.

Bam! "Are you *threatening* me? Do you *dare* threa—"

Yip!

"Hi, Zack! Hi!" Panic instantly fried my brain. I couldn't think of a single intelligent thing to say. Instead, I giggled hysterically into the phone. "How *are* you?"

I took the cordless as far into my closet as it would go without losing reception. I curled up and tried to hold the phone in the soundproofing of my armpit.

"Big bad man in his bedroom slippers!" Mom mocked my father. She was out of control. Was this about the missing couch? What did he mean it *was* his house? I'd never heard my mother stand up to my dad like this before. It was as thrilling as it was terrifying.

"I'm cool," Zack said. "I was wondering if—"

Crash! Either my mother or my father (God, I hope it wasn't Dirk) had picked up something and thrown it. I heard a grunt, a thud, and a huge crash. Juan yelped and darted down the hall.

"What's going on there?" Zack asked.

"On? What do you mean *on*? On?" I bit my lip, suddenly realizing that I, too, was on the verge of losing control.

"Uncle Randall's chair?! How *dare* you!" Mom went ballistic. Apparently, the thing that had been thrown was the old chair she'd inherited from her uncle. It was the only thing she had of value, she often said. I thought it was ugly. The tapestry seat was all threadbare and the curvy wooden legs were all scuffed. But Mom called it an "heirloom" and dusted it more than she ever dusted any of our other cruddy furniture. It sounded as though Uncle Randall's chair had been busted to bits.

"You've crossed the line, Lot," Mom wailed, part crying, part bellowing in a crazy voice I'd never heard before.

"That noise? Are you outside?" Zack asked.

Squeezing further into my closet and my armpit, I desperately tried to sound breezy as I said, "Oh *that*. Uh, that's construction. We're, uh, adding a room. A new kitchen."

"Oh." Zack didn't sound convinced.

"You want to end it? You want to end it right now?" Mom was sobbing now.

"Stop it! Stop it!" Dirk was wailing, too.

"I was wondering if we could meet tomorrow after school?" Zack said. "You know, to help me with my essay? I have a paper due the next day."

"Walk out that door and you are *never* coming back. *Never.* I'll take the house, the cars. You'll be on the streets."

Yip! Yip! Juan had returned.

Dad wasn't crying. I noticed, too, that he hadn't volunteered to take the dog or us.

"Sure," I said to Zack, my voice too high. "That'd be great. Great. Tomorrow."

"Cool. So . . ."

I could hear Dad shouting, Mom screaming, Dirk crying, and Juan Dog barking. The only thing I *didn't* hear was what Zack Nash said to me next. All I knew was that it was a question, and, in panic, I answered, "Absolutely!" He said, "Bye," and I hung up without knowing what on earth was happening with my family or what I'd just agreed to do with the boy I was now one microscopic step closer to seriously kissing.

chapter six

Nadine highlighted her hair. Without even telling me. She'd stopped by Sav-On on her way home from school, bought "Born Blonde" hair color, and locked herself in the bathroom after dinner to streak platinum peroxide through her long, already blondish, hair. Without even telling me.

"Your mom let you do this?" I asked, incredulous.

"Not exactly," she said, smoothing her stripes down in back. Then she looked at her watch, said, "Geez, the bell's about to ring," and took off for her class. I took off after her.

"What do you mean, 'Not exactly'?" I asked.

"She didn't exactly know I was going to do it. I mean, she didn't know until she saw it already done."

My jaw dropped. Is this what a potential boyfriend does to you? Turns you into a juvenile delinquent? "You did it anyway? What did she say?" I asked, breathless.

Nadine turned to me and frowned. "She said I'm grounded till my roots grow back one inch. Can you believe it? One whole inch!"

The tardy bell rang. We both sprinted to class. On the way Nadine said, "No phone, no TV, no e-mail until my hair grows an inch! My mom is such a beast." Then, just before peeling off into her third period classroom, she stopped and asked me, "Do you think an inch will grow out by Halloween? I'm hoping Curtis asks me to the Fright Dance."

"Uh. I dunno." That's all I could manage to say. It was the end of September. Halloween was a month of hair growth away. Fright Dance? Doesn't that just take the cake?

I barely made it to American History. Mr. Redfield was just shutting the door when I zoomed in.

"Glad you could join us, Miss Madrigal," he said.

Sitting down, catching my breath, I tried to focus on his lecture, but all I kept thinking about, over and over, were Nadine's blond stripes. How could she? It was so unfair. She already almost had a date to the Fright Dance? What's up with that? I'd heard all about Fernando's freshman Fright Dance. It was supposedly more fun than the prom. Part haunted house, part masquerade party, part dance—how could it *not* be totally great? But only the coolest girls went to Fright Dance with guys. The rest of us dressed up with our friends and went in a group. Fright Dance is one of the few times going with a group of girls is okay. I mean, the school year starts in September, Fright Dance is at the end of October— who could possibly have a boyfriend by then? I wanted to cry. How had this happened? How had I lost her so fast? What kind of best friend bleaches her hair without even telling you or plans to go to Fright Dance with a boy instead of you?

* * *

The walk to my new locker in Siberia felt endless. Thank heavens it was the mid-morning break. Otherwise, I'd never make it to my next class on time. My locker was at the farthest edge of campus, over by the new bungalows, along a million open-air corridors that were about as dusty as our backyard. I could barely put one foot in front of the other without sweating in the uncomfortable heat. And the last thing I wanted on my favorite, brand-new, embroidered blouse that cost one month's worth of allowance plus three weekends of babysitting was a sweat stain. Not when I was tutoring Zack Nash after school and he was tutoring me.

Fernando High School, shoved up against the foothills of the Santa Susana mountains, compensated for its lack of beauty with enormous size. All the buildings were either brown, beige, or a sort of crusty yellow. And they were spaced far apart from one another. We called it "campus" instead of "school" because, yeah, it sounded grown-up and collegelike, but also because a campus is really the grounds of a school, and Fernando High certainly covered a lot of ground. Getting from one end of campus to the other could take, like, fifteen minutes in platform sandals, ten minutes in tennis shoes. Kids with money brought fiberglass skateboards to school and showed off their zigzag moves in front of everybody. Greg Minsky never brought his skateboard.

"It'll just get ripped off," he said. But I suspected it was because he had a hard time balancing with a heavy, full backpack on his back. The guys who rode skateboards at Fernando High appeared to have more money than homework.

My mom told me the area around Fernando High is full of his-

53

tory. Like Fernando itself is the name of some Spanish king who sent missionaries to California to tame the natives and turn them into Christians. Which explains the ancient San Fernando Mission a couple of miles away. It looks totally cool from the outside, but I've never been inside because my parents keep saying, "We should go to the mission one of these days," but "one of these days" never comes. All I remember learning about the missions in junior high was that the Spaniards thought they were all holy and stuff, saving the Indians, but they actually brought lots of diseases with them that killed thousands of native Californians. Just goes to show you—forcing people to be who you want them to be is a real killer.

There is one cool thing about our little corner of the San Fernando Valley, though. It's actually a ways off campus, but the kids at Fernando High have adopted it as our own: Oakwood Cemetery. Fred Astaire and Ginger Rogers are both buried there, not next to each other, but I bet they dance together in the afterlife. If there is an afterlife. Visiting the cemetery after dark is a ghoulish pastime around here. Especially after Fright Dance on Halloween. Which makes me feel upset all over again. If Nadine and Curtis cruise the cemetery after Fright Dance, I'll just die.

Anyway.

My locker was a gazillion miles away, but I was feeling surprisingly confident in spite of my best friend vaporizing before my eyes. I knew my new blouse looked good, and I was wearing my favorite Levi's shorts, washed just enough times to be comfy. Last night I went all out and borrowed Mom's nail polish to paint my toenails Vroooom! (Translation: bright red.) Believe it or not, it looked very cool. And I blew my hair dry that morning, even though it's already straight, so it would be *super* straight. How could Zack Nash resist?

It wasn't until I was almost at my locker that my confidence disintegrated into tiny, shriveled pieces.

"Hi, Bethy."

Carrie Taylor leaned against my locker twirling her impossibly long, perfectly blond, naturally super-straight hair around one olive-oil tanned finger.

"I'm Libby now," I said, sounding retarded even to me.

Carrie just chuckled.

"I've been waiting for you . . . Libby."

"Me?"

"Yes, *you*. Why else would I walk this far? Man, is this locker a punishment or what?"

"My other locker—"

"Yeah, I heard." Carrie sounded bored as she stepped back to let me try to remember the combination to my lock. She had that effect on me. I lost my mind around her. I felt like a wart. Everything about Carrie Taylor was smooth. She didn't have a single freckle on her face—not even one bump—just skin that looked like coffee with extra cream. Her lips were naturally mauve colored. Her eyelashes were blond, and she didn't even wear mascara. And her khaki shorts, rolled up to obscenity, revealed tan legs so satiny I swear she shaved them every *hour*.

"Zack told me you're helping him with his essay after school," Carrie said.

"Yeah, well, if I can. I mean, I'll do my best." Why did I sound so guilty? Could Carrie Taylor see that I wanted to seriously kiss her boyfriend?

"That's really cool, Bethy."

I let the name thing go. "Thanks," I said, though I wasn't sure what I was thanking her for.

"I mean, you're so smart and everything."

"Thanks," I said again, though my voice sounded a bit weaker. Why was she here?

Carrie toyed with a tiny gold heart on a gold chain around her neck. Had Zack given that to her?

"I guess I'm grateful in a way," she said. "If I was smart like you, Zack would never be my boyfriend. You know how guys like him hate brainy girls."

I started to say "thanks" again, but I stopped myself. I think I'd just been insulted. Some brain. I couldn't even tell when I'd been slapped in the face. And hadn't Carrie Taylor just insulted herself? Why did it sound so good when Carrie called herself a moron?

"Well . . ." It's all I could think of to say. My locker finally opened and I had to concentrate real hard to figure out why I was there at all. Oh yeah. My Geometry book. Next class. Zack Nash and utter confusion. "Gotta go."

"Me too," Carrie said. "Cheerleading practice. Can you imagine them making us practice on a hot day like this?"

"How hideous."

"Listen to me, complaining already. I should be thankful they let me on the varsity squad at all! It's, like, *unheard* that a freshman makes varsity cheerleader. God, I am such an ingrate."

"Ingrate? That's a mighty big word for a dunce."

That's what I wanted to say. But I didn't have the nerve, not when Carrie Taylor's toe ring was just so perfectly situated on her lovely, flat, tanned middle toe. Carrie didn't need Vroooom! Her toenails and her fingernails were naturally pink, with natural white half moons edging each digit.

Instead, I said too brightly, "Well, I'm off to class." Horrified, I noticed I almost said, "classaroo." My shorts were sort of bunched up inside my thighs. I tried to dislodge them as I walked away, but they just bunched up even more.

"Oh, Bethy, I almost forgot," Carrie called after me.

I turned to face her.

"I have a message for you from Zack," she said.

Just hearing his name in connection with mine made the hairs on my freckly arm stand up. "For me?" I stammered.

"Zack is absent today, but he said to tell you he still wants to meet you after school. In the library."

"Oh. Okay. Cool."

Then Carrie nearly blinded me with her superwhite teeth, and I was left to navigate Geometry all on my own.

It felt like two hours, but it was actually only half an hour. Still, I knew in my gut that Zack Nash wasn't going to show.

"Did you miss the bus, dear?" Mrs. Kingsley, the librarian, asked me.

"No. I'm meeting someone. Or I was *supposed* to meet someone."

There were only about two other students in the library with me. There was no way I could have missed Zack, even though I checked each cubicle like five times. Eventually, Mrs. Kingsley started looking at me with pity in her eyes. That's when I decided to leave.

"If a student named Zack Nash comes in," I said to her, "could you please tell him I had other plans and couldn't wait?" It was a last-ditch attempt to salvage some dignity.

Mrs. Kingsley nodded and smiled that pity smile again. I could tell in her eyes she knew what I knew—Zack Nash had stood me up.

All the way home, I was on the verge of tears. I felt so . . . so . . . *God*, I don't even *know* how I felt. It was just this lumpy pain in my stomach, like I was a terminal loser. What was I thinking? Yeah, like Zack Nash would ever seriously (or otherwise) kiss me or even treat me like a human being.

The closer I got to home, the worse I felt. Our house had become a combat zone. My parents weren't speaking to each other. The house was full of land mines. One wrong move, one mistaken word, and our whole lives would blow. Dad had stormed out the night before, hadn't come home until it was becoming the next day. His stumble over the footstool in the family room, and subsequent slurred, curse-filled rant, woke everybody up. Though nobody moved. As ever, we braced ourselves for the hurricane, for the gale-force wind that would tear the roof off our lives at any moment.

"Libby, is that you?" Dad's voice greeted me from the living room as soon as I walked in the front door. He wasn't blotto, not yet, but I could tell he'd had a few. I sighed.

"Yeah, it's me," I said, making my way to my room.

"C'mon in here, Lib. Your friend is here."

Friend? My heart stopped. Please, oh please, if I've ever done anything good in my life, let that friend be Nadine.

"Where have you been?"

The voice was familiar. Wretchedly, sickeningly, barfingly familiar. Like looking at an awful car accident, I knew I should run the other way, but I couldn't resist. Turning, I walked toward the living room, unable to breathe. And then I saw him. An image I'd carry with me for life burned onto my eyes. There, sitting on a kitchen chair, next to my half-drunk dad, who was still in his bathrobe, slumped in a shabby, fake-leather Barcalounger, beside Uncle Randall's busted heirloom chair and the dusty, hair-balled space where the old couch used to be, in the middle of our cruddy living room and pathetic, secret life, was the boy I'd now never, ever, kiss. Now Zack Nash knew everything. There was nowhere left to hide.

chapter seven

It was a miscommunication (yeah, right), an honest mistake (uh-huh), a case of me not hearing right (oh, *puhleeese*). Carrie Taylor insisted she'd told me Zack Nash would meet me at my *house* after school.

"If I said 'library' it was a pure boo-boo," she cooed when I saw her again. "I'm so sorry if I messed you up."

I would come to believe there was nothing pure about Carrie Taylor. Nothing at all.

It was awful.

It was mortifying.

It was very nearly obscene.

Seeing Zack Nash sitting in my dumpy house with my slobbery, half-sloshed dad was the worst moment of my life.

"What do you mean where have I been? Where have *you* been?" I demanded, panic disintegrating my manners.

"I've been right here," Zack said. "Waiting for you."

Juan Dog stood quaking. *Yip! Yip!*

"How have you *both* been?" Dad asked, too slowly, completely missing the gist of the conversation. His robe fell open. He caught it just before we all saw something we'd *never* forget.

Yip! Yip!

"You've got to get out of here, Zack," I practically shrieked. "I mean, we've got to get out of here. I mean, do you still have time to work on that essay? It's not too late, is it? Is it?"

Zack looked at me slack jawed. I was obviously on the brink of hysteria. Terror, shame, guilt, humiliation all ricocheted through my head like a pinball gone berserk. My whole body went on tilt. No matter how many times I screamed Shut up! Shut up! Shut up! in my head, I was utterly unable to stop babbling.

"We should work in the kitchen. No! The family room. No! My bedroom. *No!* God, no. The backyard. No! Uh, want a soda? A soft drink of some kind?"

"Okay, sweetheart," Dad mumbled. "Do we have any Orangina?" One slipper dangled from his bare big toe. "With ice?"

Juan kept barking. *Yip! Yip!*

Suddenly Rif burst through the front door, slamming it hard. His hair was uncombed, his shoes untied. He grumbled something about global warming, then clomped heavily down the hall to his room and slammed that door, too.

Zack showed no signs of getting up. Though I couldn't blame him. I'm sure he thought my head would soon spin all the way around and I'd hurl pea soup. He looked terrorized when I lunged forward and grabbed his arm.

"C'mon!"

Yip! Yip!

"Quiet, Juan!" I screamed. Mercifully, Juan shut up. He toddled after us.

"Nice to meet you, Mr. Madrigal," Zack stammered, tripping over his feet as I dragged him into the kitchen.

"Anytime, lad," said my father.

Lad? Would the humiliation ever end? Dad was now a *leprechaun*?

As I rushed Zack from the living room, Dad called after me, "Don't forget my Orangina, Bethy."

"Betsy?" Zack asked. "Is that your real name?"

Yip! Yip!

Oh God, please take me now, I silently prayed.

Mom stored the case of Orangina she bought at Costco in the garage underneath the forty-pound bag of dog food she bought for our two-pound Chihuahua and the jumbo pack of toilet paper she bought for us.

"I'll be right back," I said to Zack, sitting him at the kitchen table. "Don't move. I mean, please just sit right there and I'll be right back. I just said that, right? I mean, hang out in the kitchen, if you would, while I get my dad's Orangina in the garage."

"Hey, what happened to the construction?" Zack asked innocently. "When my parents renovated our kitchen it took, like, months."

"Construction?"

Yip?

"The kitchen renovation you mentioned over the phone," Zack said. "All that banging."

"Ah yes, the renovation." I stalled for time. My lower lip hung like Dirk's, my brain locked in a panic freeze. I could feel circles of sweat expanding in my armpits. True, few rooms in the world needed renovation more than the Madrigal kitchen. Mom had wallpapered the eating area with Friendly's wallpaper. Not a smiley, happy wallpaper, but the *actual wallpaper* from the Friendly's restaurant chain, complete with the Friendly's name and logo. No, I am *not* kidding. The construction company she worked for had built a Friendly's in the valley and there was a roll of wallpaper left over.

"Can I take that?" Mom had asked her boss.

"To the dump?"

"No. I want to take it home."

"Why?"

"So I can wallpaper my kitchen with it."

He laughed, thinking she was joking. That's what Mom told us when she brought the large industrial roll of wallpaper home. We laughed, figured she was joking, too. A week later, we were eating every family meal in a Friendly's restaurant dining room. Mom's explanation: "Diners make me feel happy." Then she added, "Besides, nobody will see it but us."

Who would have thought Zack Nash would be sitting on one of our vinyl chairs at our faux-wood table in our Friendly's dining nook? It was simply too hideous to imagine.

"We're actually just starting construction," I explained, a trickle of sweat slowly making its way through my hair. "That's what you heard. The *beginning* of renovation. The *banging* part of it. Yeah, the, uh, constructionists won't start up here for, God, like two weeks or something. That's what they told us, anyway."

Constructionists? Ah, geez.

Zack just stared.

"Libby! My Orangina!" Dad called from the living room. At that moment, I loved him more than I could express.

"Right away, Dad!" I called out. Then I excused myself to the garage to wrestle with the Costco tower.

Only in the dark, cool dampness of the garage could I begin to breathe again. I shut my eyes, leaned against the door, inhaled deeply, and blew it out. I started to feel calmer, more human. Everything's going to be okay, I said to myself. Zack probably didn't even notice that Dad was blotto. Dressed in his robe at four in the afternoon? That could be considered artistic.

As good luck would have it, I didn't need to dismantle the Costco tower after all. I was able to wriggle my hand underneath all the piled-up stuff and pull out three Oranginas. Then, to be on the safe side, I pulled out two more just in case my dad or Zack wanted seconds. My heart was actually returning to its normal beat when I pushed through the door and made my way back into the kitchen.

Pwoosh! The pop top on the beer can sent a fine beer spray into the air. I saw my father's Adam's apple bob up and down and heard his swallow as he gulped a mouthful of brew. "Never mind about the soda, Lib."

I nearly dropped all five Orangina bottles right there in our Friendly's kitchen.

"What are you *doing* in here, Dad?"

He responded with a deep, belly burp.

"We have to study! Zack has been here too long already. We need the table. He has an essay due tomorrow." I so frantically rattled off all the reasons why my dad had to leave, I didn't noticed he'd begun to cry.

"I'm gonna miss this dump," he said, sniffing.

Zack seemed unfazed by the horror unfolding before our eyes. "My mom felt the same way," he said, gently, "before our kitchen renovation."

"Zack, we have to leave," I blurted out. "Now. Right now."

"Good times . . . so many good times . . ." Dad slapped the palm of his hand on the table so hard Zack, Juan, and I all jumped. "Right here at this very dinner table."

"Zack, you're going to get an 'F' on that essay!" I was practically screaming at him. Juan Dog got scared. *Yip. Yip.*

"Chill out." Zack stood up and slung his backpack over his shoulder. My dad tightened the terry cloth belt on his robe, stood up, too, then fell back in his chair.

"You're good people, Jackie," he slurred as his ruddy, flushed face squeezed up into another outbreak of tears.

Ah, *geez.*

Just take me now, God. A single thunderbolt to the head.

"Where are we going?" Zack asked as I shoved him out the front door.

"How about Chatsworth Park?" I suggested, my dry mouth smacking.

"Chatsworth Park? Isn't that a little far?"

"Why don't we just walk for a few minutes," I said quickly. "We can walk and talk . . . about your essay."

"Okay," Zack said dubiously.

Grateful beyond belief, I exhaled. My heart was still racing, but outside the house I felt considerably calmer. Like the stillness after a tornado twists through a trailer park, I felt strangely peaceful though wrecked. Six inches away from the boy that I loved, my emotions were too spent to freak me out.

"Good, good," I said. "Let's walk."

So we walked. We passed a 7-Eleven minimart and a bunch of kids in baggy pants hanging out by the ice machine. We passed a doughnut shop that smelled like vanilla and baked sugar, a dry cleaner that reeked of chemicals. It was hot out, but I wasn't sweating anymore. The warmth actually felt good for a change. I exhaled.

"Writing an essay is like having an argument you win," I said after we'd walked in silence awhile. "You start off stating how you feel about something or what you want to prove, then you prove it. At the end, you say, 'See? I told you I was right.'"

Zack chuckled. I loved it when he chuckled.

"What is your essay supposed to be about?" I asked.

"Passion," he answered, and a spark of electricity shot through my entire body. "We're supposed to write an essay about something we feel passionate about."

Please God, don't let his essay be about Carrie Taylor.

"I want to write about pitching," he said, "but I don't know where to begin."

"Pitching? Like in baseball?"

"Yeah, like being a pitcher and standing on the mound and knowing the entire game is in your hands. To me, that's passion."

I knew all about that. I saw Zack pitch a game once, last year. Nadine made me go to the intramural game because she had a crush on the third baseman. I barely noticed any of the players; my eyes were locked on the mound. Zack Nash stood there, in his snug uniform, twirling the baseball in his fingers, hoofing the ground with his cleats, adjusting the bill of his cap, slyly glancing over his shoulder at the base runner. Then he reached high over his head, brought his hands back down to his heart, and cata-pulted the ball across home plate. It was mesmerizing. Yeah, I knew all about the passion of pitching.

"The pitcher's mound is the center of the universe," he said quietly. "It's the top of Mount Everest. When you're up there, there's an eerie kind of silence. I mean, you can hear the crowd, but they're sort of background noise, like rain falling or some-thing. What you really hear is the catcher, speaking to you with his hands, his eyes. He knows you, everything about you. He's concentrated on your every move. He can tell if you're upset just by the way you grip the ball. He knows how to calm you down. He knows what you're going to do even before you do it. It's totally close, that relationship, like best friends. I mean, the way we communicate, the way we know each other, it's almost like *love*."

I was speechless. I wanted to be a catcher, *his* catcher. I longed to communicate silently with him, with my hands and my eyes. I wanted to drown out all the background noise and con-centrate on his every move.

"My girlfriend thinks I'm crazy," Zack said, laughing. "She says baseball is just a dumb game."

"That's because she's just a dumb blonde."

That's what I *wanted* to say. But of course I didn't. The mere mention of his "girlfriend" totally ruined the spiritual moment I was sure Zack and I had just shared. Instead I blurted out, "You don't need me, Zack." Then, frantically editing myself I added, "I mean, you don't need me to help you with your essay. You've got it all right there."

"Right where?"

"That stuff you just told me, that's poetry. That's passion. That's writing. Just write it down."

He thought for a moment. "Thanks," he said finally. "I'll do that."

"You're welcome."

I waited for more, for him to say, "I never noticed how beautiful you are and how smart. How could I have missed it?" Instead he said, "I've gotta go."

"Go?"

"I have an essay to write."

I burst into laughter—way too loud for the joke. Zack had that perplexed look on his face again.

"Thanks again, Betsy," he said.

I didn't correct him. When Zack Nash called me "Betsy" it sounded like poetry.

chapter eight

October was the month from hell at the Madrigal house.

It was the longest stretch of silence I can remember. It scared everybody. Even Juan Dog didn't dare interrupt the tension in our home with a bark or a whimper. It was that bad.

"Libby, please pass the McNuggets," Mom would say.

"Libby, when your mother is finished selecting her McNuggets, could you please pass them back to me?" Dad would say.

"Libby, when your father is finished with the honey-mustard sauce, could you please pass it to this end of the table?"

"Libby, if your mother isn't using the barbecue sauce, could you please hand it to me?"

My arm would reach right and left across the table, and I'd watch my parents not look at me or each other. My mother deliberately chewed her food as if each bite were packed with explosives. Dad washed chunks of food down his throat with mouthfuls of beer. I don't think he chewed at all. Rif kept his head down and was the last to arrive and the first to leave. This went on for days, almost two weeks, in fact. One night, overcome by the stress of witnessing the disintegration of our parents' marriage, Dirk burst into tears.

"My best friend is joining the Boy Scouts and I can't even go with him," he wailed. "You need a parent's permission slip!"

Mom said, "I'll give you a permission slip, honey."

Dad said, "Libby, if your mother is finished taking her pizza, could you please hand me another slice?"

Early Saturday morning, I was awakened by the unmistakable sound of a buzz saw coming from the garage. I know what that sound means; I watch crime TV. Petrified, I lay rigid in my bed, my heart thumping out of my chest. My God, he's done it, I thought. I listened for screams, imagined the worst. I couldn't even cry for my mom, not yet. The shock was too fresh.

Rif peered out his bedroom door just as I did. We both looked terrified. Dirk wasn't there. Had my father taken him, too? Were we next? The blood drained from my face and pooled somewhere in the lower part of my stomach. Rif whispered, "Follow me." I swallowed, followed, too scared to be left alone. We tiptoed down the hall, toward the hideous, high-pitched whine of the buzz saw. Rif held up his hand to stop me just before we reached the door to the garage. Then he asked, "Ready?"

I nodded, but I wasn't ready at all. Paralyzed by the thought of seeing what I was about to see, I clamped my eyes shut as Rif blasted open the door.

"Good morning, kids!"

Whistling and clear-eyed, Dad was cutting segments of chair spindle. Uncle Randall's chair was upside down on his work-bench, porcupined with clamps.

"Hand me that wood glue, would ya, son?" he asked Dirk.

Stunning us both, Mom appeared with a steaming cup in her hand. "Coffee, Lot?" she asked.

"Ah." He sighed, reaching to hug her. "My angel of mercy."

Clearly, they'd worked things out.

I remember every second of that day, every millisecond. My family seemed to glow around the edges. My dad was my dad again. He was funny, charming, silly. We couldn't stop smiling. Mom made lemonade and ham and cheese sandwiches from scratch.

"Just a little *snackywacky* to keep body and soul together," she chirped. She served them on a tray in the garage where Dirk was helping Dad fix Uncle Randall's chair so he could earn a Boy Scout merit badge.

I brought our old radio out and plugged it into the outlet over the workbench. Mom turned to an oldies station and danced with my father when "My Sharona" came on. Even Rif tapped his foot. I felt so happy, I wanted to cry—just burst into tears the way I sometimes do when Oprah does a story on a woman who digs herself up from the depths of despair and finds true love in a soup kitchen. I wanted to kiss every member of my family and hug them hard with my full body the way Oprah hugs her inspira-tional guests.

That night, Mom cooked dinner. And I helped.

"Could you please plug in the George Foreman, Libby?" she asked. I lit up. My brothers and I had pitched in to buy Mom a

Lean Mean Grilling Machine a couple of Christmases ago, but she had only used it once. "If only I could throw it in the dishwasher," she said, by way of lame explanation. "Who has time to hand wash a grill?"

Happily, I plugged George in and ripped up a head of lettuce for a salad. *Romaine,* not iceberg. I even made a vinaigrette from scratch. Mom marinated five chicken breasts and told me to pour five glasses of milk.

"Five?"

"Daddy's drinking milk with us tonight," she said. This time, when she said, "Daddy," it sounded perfectly right.

Everything was perfectly right. Mom asked, "Need any help with your Fright Dance costume?"

I couldn't believe she even knew about it. Stunned, I stammered, "No," and Mom walked over to me and encircled me with her arms. She stood on her tiptoes and kissed the top of my head.

"Everything's going to be okay, sweetie. You'll see."

In my mother's fleshy arms, smelling her smell, I felt like a kid again. I remembered a time she took me to a mother-daughter fashion show at a fancy department store in Encino. I wore white gloves and black patent leather shoes. She wore a pink dress that made me think of bubble gum. We ate little sandwiches that had no crusts and watched women parade by us in the most beautiful clothes I'd ever seen. Mom was beautiful, too. As I gazed up at her, I thought, When I grow up, I want to be just like my mom.

That was when we were two girls in a family of guys. We read *Family Circle* magazine together and clipped recipes. We went shopping at the mall and ate ice cream cones. That was when Dad drank only one cocktail after work, and Mom ate salads. I was young and things were simple.

It felt like we were back there again.

With the grilled chicken breasts and homemade romaine salad on the table, my family held hands in a circle and said grace. Well, Rif, Dirk, and I *mumbled* grace because we'd forgotten the words. At the end, before "Amen," Dad bowed his head and said, quietly, "Thank you for my family, this food, and the strength to be a better dad."

I nearly burst into tears.

After so long, it felt so . . . so . . . *normal.*

Then, the police came to the door.

At first, Mom was actually relieved it wasn't a bill collector.

"Does a Richard Madrigal live here?" the uniformed officer asked my parents. Mom's face abruptly fell to the floor.

"We call him Rif. My son, my younger son, my other son, couldn't pronounce 'Rich' when he was a baby, and, well, the nickname . . ." Mom was babbling.

"Are you Richard's parents?"

"What has he done?" Dad asked.

Rif leaped up from the dinner table and dashed to his room. I didn't move a muscle. I wanted to hear everything the cops were saying.

"Your son has been identified on a surveillance tape in a shoplifting incident."

"Shoplifting?"

"Apparently he took several cartons of cigarettes."

"Cigarettes?" Mom's mouth fell open. "My son doesn't smoke."

Upon hearing that, I stood up and bounded down the hall to

get Rif in his room, but he'd already escaped out his bedroom window. I saw sneaker footprints in the dirt of our backyard.

Winnie, the neighbor's dog, was barking her guts out.

Deflated, I plopped down on Rif's unmade bed. Couldn't we ever have a family dinner that wasn't a freak of nature?

The Chatsworth Police Station looks more like a library than a police station. The low, beige brick buildings are lined up neatly with one another. Law and *order*, I thought when my dad drove up with all of us in the car.

"Libby and Dirk, you stay home," Mom had said earlier that evening after Rif came home and confessed. Well, he didn't officially confess until Dad swatted him on the head and a cigarette butt shot out like a popped kernel of corn.

"No way am I staying home," I'd said.

"Me, either." Dirk was scared of going to a real-live police precinct, I could tell. But he was more scared of missing a family outing. They were so rare in our family.

So, it was about eight that night when the Madrigal family piled into the car and drove to the edge of the San Fernando Valley to the police station to turn Rif in. On the way, of course, we stopped for fast food. No one had been able to eat Mom's home-cooked meal with Rif's impending arrest stressing everybody out.

"You never know what kind of crud they're going to feed you in jail," Mom said testily to Rif. Then, to the intercom at the drive-through window, she shouted, "Four Whoppers, four large orders of fries, a chicken sandwich, no bun, four regular Cokes, and one Diet Coke."

Some things never change, even when your big brother is a perp.

In the lobby of the precinct, Dirk and I sat on a bench while my parents disappeared with Rif and a detective. They were gone for about an hour. I have to tell you, it wasn't as exciting being there as I'd imagined. I spent the first fifteen minutes examining the color head shots of past and present police chiefs. I bought Dirk another Coke from the vending machine. The rest of the time, I pretty much watched him swing his legs back and forth under the bench. Dirk said, "I sure hope I never get arrested."

I shot back, "People don't just get arrested, you numbskull. They commit a crime and they get *caught*. If you don't want to do the time, don't do the crime."

Instantly, I regretted my tone. It wasn't very sisterly, to say the least. I'd always tried to protect my sensitive little brother from my insensitive family. And here it was *me* being mean. I reached over and put my arm around Dirk's shoulder as he hung his head, still swinging his feet.

"Everything is going to be okay, you know."

He nodded unconvincingly.

"It is," I said. "I swear."

Please God, I silently prayed, let what I just said be true.

Finally, my parents emerged from the interesting section of the police station, walking behind Rif. "Community service," he grumbled, "and counseling."

"Which I've requested for the whole family," Mom said proudly.

"All of us?" I asked, incredulous. "What did *I* do?"

"A problem with one family member is a problem with the

whole family," Mom said, obviously quoting Dr. Phil. Then she marched out the door to the car.

"No it *isn't*!" I screeched, racing after her. "Rif is the thief, not me!"

Rif said, "They get you hooked on nicotine, then they won't let you buy cigarettes! It's a conspiracy to get the parks cleaned up for free."

Apparently, his community service included a trash bag and a broom in Chatsworth Park. In the car, Dad turned the ignition and pulled out of the parking lot. Mom said, "You got off light, Rif. You could have gone to jail."

"But we got off heavy!" I whined, repeating, "What did I ever do to deserve counseling?"

Dad suddenly piped up, "She's right, Dot. This isn't fair."

Mom glared at him. Buoyed by my father's resistance, I followed suit. "No. It *isn't* fair."

"In fact," said my dad, "I'm not going to do it."

"Me, either," I said. "I'm not going."

"Me, either," Dirk said, then inexplicably began to cry.

"We're all going," Mom said.

"No, we're not." Rif had jumped on the bandwagon. He crossed his arms in front of his chest.

"*You* are *definitely* going, Rif," Mom said. "It's a court order."

"Court schmort," Rif said. "The judge was on the *phone*."

"What difference does that make?" Dad asked, getting annoyed.

"If I'd been allowed to go before the judge, I could have pled not guilty on the grounds of conspiracy."

"Conspiracy! You were caught on tape shoving three cartons

of cigarettes down your pants!"

"Which I *would* have paid for, if I was *allowed* to!"

Dirk cried louder. Mom said, "This family needs help, and now is our chance."

"I'm not going," I said over and over.

"We're *all* going," Mom said firmly, "and that's an order."

"An order? An *order?*" The car suddenly got very quiet. Dirk's periodic sniffs were the only sound other than the hissing of steam shooting out of my father's ears. "The day I take orders from you, Dot, is the day you fit into a size two."

"Big bad man," my mother said mockingly to my dad.

"Not as big as your ass, my dear," he shot back.

Ah, geez.

My parents were off and running again, essentially picking up where they'd left off a few weeks earlier when Dad busted up Uncle Randall's chair. Our brief intermission of family harmony was over. The long-running Madrigal main feature — *Scream*—was playing again. Dirk, Rif, and I tried to get real small in the backseat. Well, that's not exactly right. I tried to disappear altogether. By the time we pulled into our brown driveway in front of our beige house, both my parents were seeing red. Mom leaped out of the car before it was totally stopped, slammed the door, and refused to speak to my father at all after that.

Like I said, October was the month from hell. The only bright spot—and I mean the *only* one—was Zack Nash.

chapter nine

We were casual hi-bye buddies at first.

"Hi, Zack," I'd say when I saw him standing by the drinking fountain.

"Bye, Libby," he'd say, when I was behind him as we left Geometry class.

He never said anything about my dad or his robe or his slobbery tears. I don't think he even noticed our missing couch or dirt backyard. And, after I summoned the nerve to tell him my name wasn't Betsy, he never called me it again. All of which made me love him even more.

"I got a 'B' on my essay!"

Breathless, Zack came bounding up to my Siberian locker.

"I've been looking all over campus for you," he said.

Of course, I couldn't think of anything to say back. A sappy smile was pasted on my face and I couldn't stop hearing five unbelievable words over and over in my head. Looking. All.

Over. For. You. He looked all over campus for me? For *me*?

"Thank you so much, Libby," he said. His lips were the color of raspberries. Had his teeth always been so white? I wanted to tilt my head back, lower my eyelids, part my lips, and let him thank me properly. *Seriously.*

"I owe you a Geometry session," he said.

"Forget Geometry. Just kiss me. Now. Before your moronic girlfriend shows up and asks if buffalo wings are really made from tiny, flying bison."

That's what I *wanted* to say.

"Yeah," is what I said.

"Next week, okay? After school."

"Perfect."

I was looking at his eyelashes. They were curled and long and perfect. The eyelashes of a seriously kissable boy.

We met in the school library. At my insistence.

"Hi, Mrs. Kingsley," I said, steering Zack past the librarian's desk before we went to a back cubicle to study. "I found him. Zack Nash. He was at my *house* the other day. A misunderstanding."

Mrs. Kingsley blinked slowly. I could see her trying to remember who I was. Zack clearly wondered why I was telling her this, too. His thick eyebrows were pressed down into his luscious lashes.

"We'll start studying now," I said, smiling smugly.

Zack was already halfway to a table near the back of the room. I scurried after him, popping a piece of sugarless gum in my mouth to make sure my breath was minty fresh.

"Geometry is about sizes and shapes instead of numbers." Zack dove right in. "You have to sort of *see* it more than *think* about it."

He opened his textbook. I sat next to him and opened mine. Not only was he gorgeous, he smelled of fabric softener.

"Remember the five postulates?"

"Some of the guys in da Vinci's *Last Supper*?"

"Ha-ha, Libby."

I laughed, he laughed. Amazingly, I wasn't too nervous to make a joke—dumb though it was. In fact, I felt completely calm only inches away from the boy that I loved. Had the intense stress of seeing Zack Nash in my house with my dad in his robe zapped all the fear out of me? Was this some sort of post-traumatic *relaxation* syndrome?

"The next quiz is on circumferences and congruent triangles."

I groaned.

"Don't worry. You can do this."

When Zack Nash said it, I actually believed it.

We worked together in the library for about an hour. Miraculously, Geometry began to make sense.

"That's a ninety-degree angle! And so is *that* one!"

"Right." Zack beamed and I felt beautiful.

Two days later, as Mr. Puente handed out the quizzes in class, Zack flashed me a thumbs-up. For the first time since the semester began, I felt eager to take a math quiz. At least, I didn't feel like the class dunce anymore. Not when it came to congruent triangles.

After the bell rang, as we shuffled out of class, it was all I could do to keep from flinging my arms around my hero, Zack Nash.

"I got it!" I squealed. "I saw it! You're awesome."

"I told you," Zack said, as proud as I was.

After the triumph of the Geometry quiz, our hi-byes had more depth.

"Hey," Zack said, as he passed me in the hall. This time, he nodded, too. He may have even raised his eyebrows and everyone knows what *that* means.

"See ya," I said, on my way to the bus, trying to sound as sexy as an unnurtured, genetically-challenged, angst-filled, hopelessly gaga girl can.

By freshman Fright Dance, Zack Nash and I were extremely close to actually being friends. All I needed was a little time. Luckily, I had four high school years to make him mine. *Seriously* mine.

chapter ten

It's hard to tell which was more pathetic: Nadine chasing after Curtis at the Fright Dance or Carrie chasing after Zack.

"Who are you supposed to be exactly?" I asked Zack the one moment Carrie wasn't plastered to his side. Whoever he was, he was *gorgeous.* My heart pounded with the beat of the dance band on the gymnasium stage. Or was it being so close to him?

"I'm Ga—"

Carrie, spotting Zack about to utter a word without her, dove to his side. She tucked her hand into his, nestled up to him, and shouted, "What are you two talking about? Algebra?"

"It's *Geometry,* you idiot."

That's what I wanted to say. I also wanted to mention that I'd gotten an "A" in Pre-Algebra, and would probably get another "A" in Algebra next year, but that would have sounded as desperate as she did. Ever since Carrie tried to sabotage my tutoring session with her boyfriend, I'd seen her in an entirely different light. Not a flattering pink glow, either. More like a deep, envious green. She'd started waiting for Zack outside Geometry class, and if she'd see me happen to walk out with him, she'd make some cheesy remark like, "You still need help with your homework, Bethy?" No matter how many times I told her my name was Libby, she never got it right. I could tell Zack was embarrassed. I could also tell Carrie was totally jealous, which was pretty laughable. I mean, she had him body and soul; I had him for quadrilaterals. She could seriously kiss him whenever she wanted to. I had to make do with wishing, hoping, praying, and pleading with the universe that Zack Nash would one day dump Carrie Taylor, then turn to me and say, "You're *it*. You're the only girl I want." Yeah, right.

"I was just asking Zack who he was supposed to be tonight," I said to Carrie at Fright Dance.

"*We* are Gwen Stefani and Gavin Rossdale!" she chirped. Zack rolled his eyes. So *that's* why Zack had his hair slicked back.

"I couldn't think of anything," he mumbled apologetically.

"That's why you have me," Carrie said, kissing his neck and nibbling his earlobe. Now I rolled my eyes. Zack looked about as comfortable as a boy buying his first condom.

"And who are you supposed to be?" Carrie asked me as soon as Zack's earlobe was out of her mouth. "Einstein?" She giggled.

"I'm Betty. Betty Rubble. Nadine is Wilma Flintstone."

Zack chuckled. God, I love it when he chuckles. Carrie said, "*Très* Stone Age."

"Thanks," I said. "We wanted costumes that really rock."

Zack laughed out loud. Man, I love it when he laughs out loud. Oddly, I felt calm again. Seeing Zack without losing my power of speech, going to my first freshman dance, wearing a gigantic blue bow in my hair — it all felt incredibly *normal*. Was it possible that my statement to Dirk in the police station really was true? Everything really *was* going to be okay?

"Let's dance!" Carrie tugged Zack onto the dance floor, and I watched him self-consciously sway back and forth while she wiggled obscenely all over him. Oh, brother. She's such a show-off. When being beautiful is just about all you have to offer the world, I guess it feels mighty insecure. I felt sorry for her. (Okay, I *tried* to feel sorry, but all I really felt was mad that she was such a conniving, back-stabbing you know what.)

Fright Dance was totally cool. I had to hand it to the decorating committee. Before you could get into the gym, you had to pass through the Haunted Corridor. It was completely dark except for the black lights that flashed each time thunder roared. Somebody had the majorly ingenious idea of hanging a million pieces of string from the ceiling, just long enough to tickle the top of your head and face and freak you out. They played lines from scary movies, like the one where Hannibal "the Cannibal" Lecter purrs, "I'm having someone over for dinner tonight."

But what almost made me run home screaming was the "Guts" initiation at the end of the Haunted Corridor. If you had the guts to blindly put your bare hand into three dark buckets, you were allowed into the dance. Each bucket was covered in a black sheet with a hand-sized slit in it. The first was labeled EYE-BALLS. Every girl before me who stuck her hand in screamed. The guys acted tough, but I could tell they wanted to scream, too.

"You go first." Nadine, a huge rawhide bone twisted into her hair, dug her fingernails into my arm. My heart was pounding so loudly I had my own internal thunder. Taking a deep breath, I shoved my hand into the blackness and nearly gagged. Inside, I could feel gooey, slimy, round balls—lots of them. I pulled my hand out as quickly as I put it in.

Nadine did the same, only adding a bloodcurdling shriek.

The second bucket, INTESTINES, was just as slimy and gooey. By the time I reached the third, PUS, I couldn't wait to yank my hand out and run to the restroom to wash all the "guts" off.

"Peeled grapes, spaghetti, and cream of wheat."

That was the consensus in the bathroom. Still, everybody scrubbed the "guts" off their hands and felt queasy until the shimmying and sweating of the first big dance of the year made us all forget.

"Have you seen Curtis?" a breathless Nadine, aka Wilma Flintstone, asked me as she rushed off the dance floor. The bone in her still-striped hair was flopped over to one side. She tugged at the top of her leopard-print tube dress.

"How could I see Curtis? Can anyone see Curtis?"

"Ha-ha, Libby." Curtis had arrived at Fright Dance as the Invisible Man. Which meant he wrapped a gauze bandage around his head, with two eye slits and a mouth slit, and he wore one of his dad's old hats. Each time I *did* see Curtis, he was unraveling more and more.

"I haven't seen him lately," I said to Nadine.

She groaned. "My mom is picking us up in an hour!"

Nadine's hair hadn't grown out an inch before the big Halloween Fright Dance at Fernando High. But it was almost there, so her mom relented and let her go to the dance . . . with *me.* Mrs. Tilson drove us to the gym, and planned to pick us up at eleven-thirty sharp. Which completely messed up Nadine's plan to seriously kiss Curtis at midnight.

"You're not Cinderella," I told her. "You could kiss him at eleven."

Exasperated, Nadine whined, "You don't understand."

She said that a lot lately, which really ticked me off. Just because one friend almost has a boyfriend doesn't mean the other can't understand what it's like. If explained properly, that is.

"Try me," I said testily.

"A group of us planned to go to Oakwood Cemetery after the dance."

Oh. "A group?" I asked.

"You're invited, of course. I mean, if you won't feel left out."

As I glared at my best friend, I made a mental note: *I, Libby Madrigal, do solemnly swear never to make my girlfriend feel bad about not having a boyfriend.*

"It doesn't matter anyway, Nadine," I yelled over the music that had just started up again. "Your mom is picking us up at eleven-thirty, so neither one of us can go." Then I added, "I'm going to find someone to dance with before the night is over."

And I left. Hoping to find Greg Minsky or some other guy who felt like dancing with a prehistoric girl who wore a chunky choker made of giant Styrofoam beads that were painted to look like rocks.

"Wanna dance?" Greg Minsky, Old Faithful, held out his hand. He was dressed as Bill Gates, which pretty much meant that he looked like he always did.

"Yeah," I said. "Let's dance."

Greg asked, "Want to go to Oakwood Cemetery with me at midnight?"

Nadine sulked all the way home in her mother's car. For some reason she was annoyed with me because her mom refused to let her go to the cemetery with Curtis. Like I could've convinced her mom to let her stay out past eleven thirty if only I'd tried.

I didn't let it bother me. I knew Nadine would be fine in the morning. So I leaned my head against the window, thought about how kind Greg Minsky is, how fun Fright Dance was, how cute Zack Nash will always be, and how my life was finally, finally starting to feel sort of okay.

"Thank you, Mrs. Tilson," I said as she pulled up in front of our house and tossed me an air kiss like she always does.

"Good night, sweetheart," she said.

"Good night, Nadine," I called into the backseat. Nadine just grunted.

The lights were all on inside our house. It looked rather cozy, lit up like that. I felt happy, actually glad my parents were still up so I could tell them about the Haunted Corridor.

"Elizabeth?"

Mom called me from the living room as I walked through the front door. I was just about to tell her for like the millionth time that it's Libby when I walked into the living room and noticed the whole family was there. Dirk, Rif, my parents, and Juan.

"What's wrong?" I asked, my stomach plummeting to the floor.

That's when Dad dropped the bomb.

chapter eleven

Dad was stone-cold sober on a Friday night, which should have been my first clue that our lives were about to change forever. Rif was home before midnight on Halloween, which should have been my second.

Dad took a deep breath, then said, "We're moving."

No one said a word. Not a peep. Had we heard him right?

"Moving?" I asked.

Dirk said, "Huh?"

Rif said, "We're moving? A new house? For real?"

"Moving?" I repeated. The knot in my stomach tightened.

"Yes. Moving."

Stunned, nobody moved at all. Mom looked down at her hands and quietly patted her Press-On nails.

"For *real*?" Rif repeated.

"For real," Dad said.

"Cool!"

"That's incredible!"

"My own room!"

"We're finally leaving this dump!"

Dirk and Rif whooped and hollered. Rif held up his hand and Dirk slapped a high five. I looked at my mother, who was now slowly rotating her wedding band around and around her finger. Instinctively, I reached down and gripped the seat of the kitchen chair Mom had brought into the living room for me to sit on.

"To Barstow," Dad said abruptly. Then he plopped down on his Barcalounger with a loud *thunk.*

"Where?" Dirk's lower lip glistened.

Mom fixed her stare on the dust bunnies that were still huddled together where the couch once was. Rif just sat there and stared into space. I suddenly gasped, realizing only then that I'd been holding my breath.

"What?" I burst out. "Why?!"

"This is a grown-up decision that your father and I had to make," Mom said. "I'm sorry that your lives will be disrupted, but there's no other choice. We'll pack up the house this weekend and move early Monday morning."

Early Monday morning. Those three words echoed in my head. Early. Monday. Morning. I wouldn't have the chance to say good-bye to anybody at school?! What about Nadine? What about Zack? What about congruent triangles? How could this be happening?

"No way," I said.

Dirk asked, "Is Barstow a street near us?"

"I'm not going." I crossed my arms firmly in front of my chest.

"Barstow is a city, you idiot," Rif snapped at Dirk. "It's about halfway between here and Las Vegas."

My mother glared at him. How did he know that?

"I don't care where it is," I said. "I'm not moving. I'll live with Nadine."

"If Libby lives with Nadine, can I have her room?" Dirk asked.

Now I glared at Dirk. Is that all I meant to my little brother? I felt like shoving a dust bunny up his nose. But I was too upset to do anything.

Disrupted? Had my mother apologized for *disrupting* our lives? Wouldn't *ruining* our lives be more accurate? Why Barstow? And why *now*, just as Zack Nash and I were on the road to becoming the friends that would eventually lead to becoming the serious kissers?

"What's going on?" I asked, near tears. "You can't just dump this on us!"

"Hey, I'll be sprung from community service," Rif said, grinning. "Cool."

"Sometimes adults have to make difficult, adult decisions," Mom said. Dad memorized his slippers.

My eyes nearly popped out of my head. They pick *now* to act like adults? What about last month when I needed a ride to the library and Dad suggested I hitchhike? Or the time I asked Mom the difference between a French kiss and an American kiss and she totally bailed on the truth by telling me that the French only kiss *cheeks*?

"I don't understand what's going on!" I repeated, my voice becoming desperate and whiny.

"There's nothing to understand. We're moving on Monday

and that's that." Dad sighed and stood up. "It's late. We should all get some sleep."

Nadine spent the weekend at my house sobbing. "It can't be true! Tell me it's not true!"

"It's true."

"It *can't* be true!"

"It is." I was numb. I moved like a robot around my room, throwing stuff into cartons without caring if it broke or not. My life was over. Why should I care if I busted a CD player?

"How could you do this to me?" Nadine wailed. "What about our serious kisses?"

That's when I started to cry. "You'll have to have yours without me."

"It won't mean as much if I can't tell you about it."

"Call me. If phones work in the armpit of the world." I sniffed hard and threw my reading lamp into the box.

By Sunday evening, the only things left to pack were the sheets on my bed and my toothbrush. Like zombies, Nadine and I left the Chatsworth house and wandered the streets of our neighborhood in an emotional daze.

"I need you to do something for me, Nadine," I said, as it began to get dark.

"Anything. You name it."

Stopping on the sidewalk, I faced my best friend and took a deep breath. "Will you please tell Zack I said good-bye?"

"Zack Nash? The math guy?"

"Yeah. Tell him what happened, okay? Tell him I won't ever forget hi—"

Greg Minsky suddenly appeared behind me on the sidewalk. He clamped his hands over my eyes, which he always did, which always annoyed me. His palms were clammy. He held on way too long, after I shouted, "Greg! Let go!" a million times. Pressing his body to my back, he wriggled with me. I could smell his Right Guard deodorant.

"Greg! Let *go!*" Really, I was in no mood.

"Let go of her, Greg. *God!*" Nadine gave him a little shove.

Releasing me, he asked, "Is it true?"

I ran my thumb under my bottom lashes, adjusted my disheveled shirt. "I hate when you do that."

"I hate when you do that." Greg mimicked me in a sappy, singsong voice. Boys are so immature. "Libby, is it true?"

"Yeah. It's true," I said.

His face fell. "Man," he said.

"I know. It sucks."

"Man!" For a second I thought Greg Minsky was going to cry. Hanging his head, he jammed the toe of his sneaker into a crumbling crack in the concrete. I felt awful. I liked him, but he liked me *that* way. Story of my love life. I mean, Greg's a nice guy, but I can't get past the zit clusters on either side of his chin and his unibrow. Not that I'm Miss America. It's just that I've never been able to drum up an attraction to him. I knew I'd never want to seriously kiss Greg Minsky. Never.

"Here," he said, crowding Nadine out and shoving a letter at me. I felt queasy, didn't know what Greg Minsky had to say—in a letter, no less. So I just stood there. If I didn't touch it, I didn't have to read it, right?

"Take it," he said. Sighing, I reached out and took it.

"Read it," he commanded.

"You want me to read it now? Like, in front of you?"

"Yeah." That serious action was going on in his face again. Like the time he'd planted the slobbery kiss on me. Nadine stepped back, sniffed. I felt like I'd swallowed a shovel full of mud. Obviously he wasn't going to budge. So I opened it. Right there in front of him.

Greg Minsky had written me a poem.

Once a Life
Two souls floating, searching,
*   passing in the dark night.*
One soul turning, seeing.
Who's there?
Is it you?
No answer.
Hello?
Silence.
The room is empty.
It's cold and colorless.
The walls are bare.
The only sound is the hollow echo of a beating heart.

Instantly, I felt like I always feel when I read a poem—like a total moron. I didn't get it. Was he saying that we were two souls passing in the night? Was his heart hollow, or mine? And, what, he expected me to concentrate on deciphering poetry with him staring at me like that?

"Get it?" he asked.

"Of course," I lied. "It's beautiful."

"It's a going-away present," he said. "For you."

"It's beautiful." I racked my brain for something else to say, but what else could I say?

The three of us stood there in awkward silence until Nadine sniffed again and said, "I'm so sorry, Lib. I've gotta go. Curtis is supposed to call."

"I should go, too," Greg said. "I have homework."

My two friends hugged me hard. Nadine kissed my cheek and told me she loved me; Greg, thankfully, didn't do either.

"Call me as soon as you can!" Nadine said. Then she added, "I can't deal with saying good-bye."

"Me, either," I said.

Both of my friends promised to visit as soon as they could drive. Then suddenly, just like that, they left. I watched them grow smaller and smaller on the sidewalk, looking back only once.

part two
barstow

chapter twelve

At first, I wept dramatically in the backseat of the Corolla, clutching a wadded-up Kleenex to my red, runny nose. But each time I wailed, Juan Dog lifted his little head and wailed with me.

"Mom, how could you dooooo this!" I bellowed.

Ahhhooooooo! Juan imitated me. *Oooh, oooh.*

Juan's howl made Mom, Dirk, and Rif laugh, which really made me mad. So, eventually, I let the tears flow soundlessly down my cheeks. I suffered in the loudest silence I could muster.

I'd seen the outskirts of Barstow before. On TV, when the new rovers landed on Mars and dune-buggied around and sent those orange pictures back to us. That's what Interstate Fifteen to Barstow looked like. *Mars.* Only without the orange color. As far as the eye could see was dirt and sand and scruffy scrub dotting the planetary landscape. As we drove further into oblivion, I felt so low I could walk under a snake with a beehive hairdo. There wasn't even a Burger King. I mean, you could *die* out there.

"You've got to be kidding." It was all I could say between bursts of tears. Over and over, "You have *got* to be kidding me."

"It's a desert, honey," Mom said by way of explanation.

"No way."

"Really, it's the Mojave Desert."

"I know it's a desert! No way am I living in the middle of a desert. What's going on? Why are we here?"

Mom ignored my questions, just as she'd done for the past hour. After fourteen years of watching her not tell us the truth about all kinds of stuff, I knew she could easily not tell us why we were moving to Barstow for the entire car ride there. Which is exactly what she did (and didn't) do. Stubbornly, she stared through the windshield, following Dad in the U-Move truck, with Rif, Dirk, Juan Dog, and I squished into her car. No one wanted to drive with Dad because the U-Move wasn't air-conditioned. Even in November, even before noon, it was hotter than baked asphalt.

We drove forever on the freeway. At first, it was bumper-to-bumper traffic, one driver per car, cell phone in one hand, coffee mug in the other—the typical southern California commute. Angelenos would rather spend hours in traffic than be caught dead riding a bus. Mom didn't seem to care, settled her *fannywannydingo* into the car seat, and propped her elbow on the windowsill. I leaned my head against the window and let Juan lick the tears off my face.

By the time we reached Pasadena, the traffic had thinned out and the U-Move became a small square ahead of us. At the junction to Interstate Fifteen, Dad was hardly visible, he was so far ahead.

"Do you think he's trying to ditch us?" Rif asked, joking.

Mom barely smiled. She said, "Apparently we'll have to make it there on our own."

Briefly lifting my head from the window, I blew my nose.

By the time the landscape became lunar, we'd driven about two hours. I was cried out, exhausted by despair. Fernando High, Nadine, Zack Nash—they all seemed a gazillion miles away. Juan Dog was softly snoring on my lap. Dirk opened the back window and pelted us all with sand and heat.

"Shut the window, you moron," Rif snapped. The sweltering, overhead sun made Chatsworth seem balmy. The dry, hot wind made everyone squint. Quitting smoking hadn't been easy on Rif or us. He was in a perpetual foul mood, and he dragged everybody down with him.

"*Plants* don't even live here," I moaned, looking at the desolation stretching out in every direction.

"*You're* the moron," Dirk said to Rif, rolling the window back up.

"We stay on this road, right?" Mom asked Rif. Dad was long gone.

After gazing through the windshield, Rif concluded, "There's no *other* road."

So we drove. Eventually we saw a flicker of white, then neon, then what looked like a mall up ahead. "It's a *mirage*, right?" I asked haughtily.

"Outlets!" Mom's face lit up. "In-N-Out Burger! Kids, look! Del Taco! Shall I pull off?"

"No," said Rif. "Turn around."

My sentiments exactly. Mom said, "We'll scope out the

outlets another time. We're almost there!"

"Almost *no*where," I said. Mom merrily continued to ignore us. She pulled off the freeway, followed the signs to Barstow. Which I noticed wasn't necessary. Rif was right—Barstow was the middle of absolutely nowhere. It's an old, medium-sized town surrounded by endless, flat Californian desert. The only way you'd miss it is if a humongous tumbleweed blew into town and got stuck on one of the ugly brown stucco buildings.

Mom saw it differently. Turning onto Main Street she chirped, "Oooh, look down there at the old railroad station! Look at the quaint shops!"

I said, "Oooh, look at the tattoo parlor."

"And look, Mom, body piercing!" said Rif.

"Military surplus."

"Knives, new and used!"

Mom's *look* was a knife, a dagger, actually, catapulted into the backseat. We shut up, suffered in silence. Juan, shaking, looked up at me, then out the window as Mom drove through the dreariest downtown I'd ever seen. The women looked like truck drivers, the men looked like Hell's Angels. The whole dirt-brown town seemed like time had forgotten it entirely. Butch Cassidy and the Sundance Kid could have been hiding out there for fifty years and no one would have bothered to look.

"Can't you feel the history here?" Mom squealed. "This used to be part of old Route Sixty-six!"

"Where's the new house?" Even Dirk was getting impatient.

"Look at the cute McDonald's! It's built into railroad cars!"

We all groaned at that one. Even the McDonald's looked old.

"Are we almost there?" I asked, dejected. I couldn't wait to lie facedown on my bed until college.

"We have to make one quick stop first," Mom said.

Now, we groaned even louder.

Mom consulted a crumpled piece of paper she pulled from her purse, kept driving her one-woman tour. "A Wal-Mart! Did you kids see the Wal-Mart?"

"A trailer park!" said Rif sarcastically. "Did you kids see the trailer park!"

With that, Mom flipped on her blinker and turned left into the trailer park's front entrance, underneath the arched sign that read WELCOME TO SUNSET PARK.

"Ha-ha, Mom," I said.

"Har-de-har-har," said Rif. "We get the joke. You don't have to continue the white trash tour."

Mom disregarded the howls of her young. She drove down the little streets of the trailer park, past white rock lawns, brown rock lawns, beige rock lawns, green Astro Turf, metal awnings, "patio" tables made of cinder blocks, ceramic guard dogs, and row after row of large rectangular metal trailers.

"Are we even allowed in here?" Dirk asked. Mom said nothing, just kept driving. The paved streets were covered in desert sand.

"There's a communal pool," she said. "A rec room. Look! A tree!"

Rif and I peeked at each other and instantly knew the score. Mom had gone mad. She'd seat-belted herself into an old Toyota and chosen Barstow, of all places, to lose her marbles.

"Feel like an ice cream *coney-woney*, Mom?" I asked gingerly.

Suddenly, the car stopped with a lurch. "Eureka." Mom

sighed. Stunned, we watched her release her seat belt, unlock the car door, and reach for her purse. Rif and I simultaneously turned our heads to stare out the window. The abrupt stop had engulfed us in a dust cloud. It took a few moments to settle down, but out of the grit emerged the figure of a woman, floating toward us, dressed in a flapping orange caftan, weighted down with a thick turquoise necklace.

"Nana!" Mom cried out.

Who?!

Nobody moved. We sat there, flabbergasted. Except Mom, who heaved herself out of the Toyota and ran in small baby steps across the gravel road to *kiss, kiss* the wrinkly old woman with her arms extended. My brothers and I just stared at the two of them.

Yip.

"Kids, come meet your grandmother!"

No one stirred. As far as I knew, all my grandparents were dead.

Yip. Yip!

"Come on, gang!"

Yip! Yip.

"You keep sitting in that car you're going to turn into three fried eggs!"

Yip! Yip! Yiiip!

If Juan Dog wasn't licking his lips in that way that let me know he had to go to the bathroom real bad, I never would have left the car. I would have refused to budge until my mom got back in the car, deserted the old lady, and drove us home to

Chatsworth where we belonged. I'd learned from studying the civil rights movement in school how powerful passive resistance could be. Dead weight in the back of a two-door sports coupe would be near impossible to dislodge.

Yiiiip! Yiiipppppp!

"All right, you little runt," I snapped at Juan. Rif opened the passenger door and Juan leaped out. Slowly, the three of us unfolded out of the car.

"You must be Richard," the woman said to Rif, shaking his hand.

"We call him Rif," Mom said.

"And you must be Dirk," she said to Dirk. Dirk shyly hung his head and smirked. "Yeah." He giggled. Rif disappeared behind the trailer.

"And you . . ." She wafted toward me like a giant orange manta ray. "You must be Elizabeth."

"Bethy," said Mom.

"Libby!" I shot my mother an incredulous look.

"Bethy Libby," said Nana. "How unique!"

"It's *Libby.* Period."

"Libby Period? Is that like Cher?"

Oh, brother. I just looked at her. Mom stepped in. "Nana, our Elizabeth prefers to be called Libby. For now."

"Of course!" said Nana. "Libby suits you perfectly. Libby Period is so . . . *cumbersome.*"

The elderly woman cupped my face in her hands and stared at me. Her eyes were watery but an intense contact-lens blue. In the blinding sun, her short, spiky hair was so red it was almost violet. Each finger on her bony, speckled hands was ringed with blobs of silver and coral. Her fingers clacked when she moved them.

"Absolutely magnificent," she said as she hugged me. I tensed.

"I don't mean to be rude," I said into her shoulder, "but who are you?"

Pulling back, the woman teared up and bit her lower lip. "Your parents never spoke of me? Never showed you any photographs?"

I shook my head. Mom looked down at her chubby toes.

"I'm your father's mother, Libby. I'm your *grandmother.*"

I just stared. Clearly, this was some kind of trap. Even the worst parents in the world wouldn't deny their kids a nana. Would they?

"By the way," my, uh, grandmother said, sniffing, "where's my son?"

"He'll be here soon," Mom answered without looking up. "He had a few, um, errands to run."

The old woman's face fell. "Oh, well." She sighed. "I've waited twenty years to see him. What's twenty minutes more?" Then she turned to us and said, "No sense waiting for him in the heat. Come inside, my darlings. I've waited a whole lifetime to meet you."

Rif rejoined us in front of the trailer, squirting Binaca into his mouth. As he passed me, I could smell that he hadn't quit smoking after all. He followed "Nana" and Dirk through the metal door of her trailer. Mom stood in the street looking for Dad's U-Move. I didn't budge. I mean, the woman was a complete stranger. My grandmother? Living in the same *state* all these years? If it was true, my parents were either heartless or psychotic. I didn't know whether to feel furious or turn myself in to Social Services.

"Come on in, Libby!" the old lady said at her trailer door. "I won't bite."

I just stared at her.

"I swear. No biting whatsoever."

I had to believe her. What other choice did I have?

chapter thirteen

"Let me get this straight. My grandmother *isn't* dead?"

Mom and I were alone in the searing heat outside my newly discovered nana's trailer. No way was I going inside until I knew the truth.

"Not exactly," Mom said, her yellow patent leather purse dangling on her forearm.

"Not *exactly*? Is she a clone? A robot? A mirage?"

The hotter it got outside, the more heated I felt inside. A line of sweat made its way down my flushed cheek, stopping at my gritted teeth. Glaring at my mother, I added, "Is the lady in that trailer Nana's long-lost twin?"

"Shhh! She'll hear you."

"Hear what? That you were just kidding when you told us she died before I was born?"

Mom draped one fleshy arm around my shoulder and led me

down Nana's dusty street. Each passing second made me madder and hotter.

"The truth is," Mom said in a low voice, "your father and his mother never got along."

Wriggling out from under her sweaty arm, I snapped, "So?"

"So, it was easier for him to pretend that his mother had passed away."

"Easier?"

"You know, because he didn't want to talk to her."

Stunned into silence, I felt the trickle of sweat drip off my chin.

Seriously, I could not believe what I was hearing. Though I should have. It was so . . . so *typical.* How many years had we lived with my dad's bad behavior? How often had we all pretended he wasn't drunk when we knew he was? Of course my parents would rather deprive us of a grandparent than deal with reality! Avoiding the truth is what they do best. Our family is one big fake out. Even our last name: Madrigal. A madrigal is a musical love poem. Get *out.* Our family is *so* not a musical love poem. We're more like a CD that was left out on the pavement in a Barstow summer.

"When your grandfather died," Mom continued, "your dad had sort of, um, a big fight with his mom."

Hands on my hips, I asked, "What kind of a fight?"

"A *family* sort of fight."

"What does that mean? The silent treatment for twenty years?"

"Exactly my point! Your father didn't want the anger to simmer for years, so he decided it was better for the whole family if he pretended his mom had passed on."

I gaped at her. "Better for who?"

"Whom," Mom corrected me.

"Better for *whom*?" The word "whom" hurtled out of my mouth like an angry dust storm. "Better for us to grow up without a grandmother? Wouldn't it have been better for Dad to get over it? Apologize? Do what he had to do to bring the family *together*? Isn't that what parents are supposed to do?"

Mom resumed looking for Dad's rental truck.

Images of childhood birthday parties, Christmas mornings, Thanksgiving dinners—all the times it would have been cool having a grandmother—flashed through my mind. Was she someone I could have talked to without violating the family's shhh-don't-tell policy?

The trailer door opened with a loud creak and my grandmother—not a twin nor a clone but the real deal—poked her head out and chirped, "Lunch is almost ready!" Then she popped back in and shut the metal door.

Emotionally overloaded, my head felt like a wasp's nest. I could almost feel the synapses in my brain misfiring. I wanted to either scream or crumple into a heap. I wanted to go home. I missed Nadine and staring at the back of Zack Nash's creamy neck in class. I even missed Ostensia and her stinky nachos. What was going on? Why me? Just as my life had finally begun to feel normal, I'm kidnapped to a hot, sandy street in the middle of nowhere, about to eat Spam or Velveeta or whatever else they call "food" in a trailer park with a woman I've never met, who gave birth to my father and just may have made my life easier if I'd been allowed to know she existed.

Life more than sucks.

Suddenly, a new image flashed through my brain. Panic radiated from the center of my chest, down my arms, and out my fingertips. I wheeled around to face my mother, grabbed both of her flabby upper arms, and gasped, "We're not moving into Nana's trailer, are we, Mom?"

Mom laughed out loud. "Don't be silly. Do you think we would do that to you?"

Without waiting for an answer, Mom waddled toward my grandmother's trailer, saying, "Let's go in. I'm starved."

Entering my new nana's trailer was an out-of-body experience. It was like passing through the flames of hell into air-conditioned heaven. It was *gorgeous.* I couldn't believe my eyes.

"Isn't this the biggest trailer you've ever seen?!" Dirk rushed toward us as Mom and I walked through Nana's front door.

"We call them *mobile homes,"* Nana said. "Though the only thing that's mobile around here is the garden gnome in my front yard, and technically, he just fell over."

Dirk was right. It was huge. My family stood in the center of a modern, sleek, stainless steel kitchen. Polished copper pots hung from the ceiling; a huge butcher-block island sat beneath them.

"Is that one of those Sub-Zero refrigerators?" Mom sputtered.

"Yes! Food *never* goes bad!"

I didn't have a clue what a Sub-Zero was, but Nana was beaming. My brothers and I clung to one another like a chain gang. We gaped open-mouthed at my grandmother like she was an archaeological find. Which, of course, she kind of was.

The smell was unbelievable—garlic, roasted meat, melted

butter. My stomach erupted in gurgles and growls. Mouth-watering concoctions were simmering on the eight-burner stove. Nothing even *close* to Spam and Velveeta. In the center of the surprisingly large, open space, an oval pine table was set with gold-rimmed porcelain and glistening crystal glasses. I'd never seen anything as classy before. The kitchen belonged in a magazine. The rest of the trailer must be awesome. Already, it was much nicer than our crummy Chatsworth house.

"My goodness," Mom said, as flabbergasted as I was. "Can we have the grand tour?" Her purse still dangled on her arm.

"Absolutely." Drying off her hands, Nana turned away from the sink to face her four relatives. Standing still, she swept her arms through the air. "*Voilà!* This is it."

"This is it?" Rif asked.

"Lovely!" Mom swallowed.

"You live in a *kitchen*?"

"Rif!" Mom pinched the back of his arm. "It's *lovely*!"

It was lovely, but it was also true. Nana's trailer was one big, gleaming, air-conditioned kitchen.

"I've always wanted a gourmet kitchen," she explained, "so I gave myself one. I tore down the walls and said what the heck! You only live once. Why not live near the refrigerator?"

Nobody said a word. Was she joking?

"You sleep in the *dishwasher*?" Rif asked, chuckling. Mom smacked the back of his head, and we all gasped when a cigarette butt shot out.

"Rif!" Mom snapped, snatching the butt off the floor and shooting him an angry look.

"It's quite all right," Nana said, oblivious to the fact that my

brother had just been busted for smoking. "My bed is over here."
She led our huddle around the wall-mounted TV/VCR to a large
oak armoire behind the dining room table. Opening the door, she
showed us her Murphy bed, tucked neatly inside, flat up against
the wall.

"Cool," said Dirk.

"The bed is on springs. It comes right down when I'm ready
to go to bed, and pops back up in the morning."

"You never have to make it?" Dirk asked.

"Never."

"Awesome."

"And I can lie in bed and eat off the dining room table if I
want to!"

"Lovely," Mom said again. Her purse slid down her arm. "Is
there a . . . uh, restroom?"

"I use the sink."

We froze in horror. "Just kidding," Nana said. She flung her
head back and howled. "That always scares 'em. The bathroom is
over there." Nana walked over to another oak armoire across the
room and opened the door. Inside was a tiny shower stall, a toilet,
and a small sink. "It was featured in *Trailer Life*! A friend of mine
designed this for me. Isn't it fabulous?"

"Just lovel—" Mom's purse hit the floor with a *thunk*. She left
it there while she stuffed herself into the armoire and closed the
door.

Suddenly, we heard a scratching sound at the front door.

"Juan!" I screeched.

"The neighbor's grandson? Invite him in," said Nana.

Diving for the door, I swung it open and saw Juan Dog

looking up at me pathetically, trembling on the welcome mat, his huge eyes misty.

"Oh, baby, I'm so sorry I forgot you!" A trio of poops sat a few feet away like three big Hershey's Kisses. I scooped Juan into my arms and kissed his head. "Nana, do you have a Baggie?"

Nana spotted Juan. "My, what do we have here?" she asked, stroking his elephantine ears.

"This is our Chihuahua, Juan Dog," I said.

"He's adorable! But you don't have to keep him in a Baggie, Libby. I have a vacuum cleaner."

I gaped at her. Then, I sighed. Of course my grandmother was a nut job! Why would it be any other way?

Suddenly, I envisioned the "big fight" my dad had with his mom:

Dad: "I don't wanna sleep in a kitchen!"

Nana: "Then sleep in an armoire!"

Dad: "Why can't we be normal?"

Nana: "We are normal! Now, put the dog back in the Baggie!"

Swallowing hard, I held Juan and tore off a sheet of paper towel.

"I'll be right back."

Outside Nana's trailer—mobile *schmobile,* no matter how beautiful it was, it was still a *trailer*—I cleaned up after Juan, threw it in the nearest trash can, and decided to skip lunch. Food smelling that good was too dangerous. It had an obese aroma. Better to not know what I was missing. Even if it was only one lunch, I couldn't risk it. Especially now that I had the genetic threat of becoming a woman who *lived* in a kitchen!

I decided to walk off my hunger. After all, we were moving into a new house that night. Which, of course, meant only one thing in our family—extra large, extra cheese, pepperoni pizza.

The Barstow heat was almost unbearable. It fried the inside of my nostrils each time I inhaled. The asphalt was squishy beneath my feet. Juan lay draped over my arm, either dead asleep or passed out. Briefly, I wondered if my family even noticed I was gone. Probably not.

The whole trailer park looked like a bizarre metal cult. Lined up next to one another, on the diagonal, each trailer was pretty much a copy of its rectangular neighbor. They were separated by bulbous septic tanks and boxy air-conditioning units. I could hear television sets blaring and the unmistakable violins of daytime TV. Someone peeked at me from behind a lace curtain, but snapped it shut as soon as I peeked back.

Except for the curtain peeker, Nana's street, Paradise Way, was deserted. The lack of life was eerie, like I really was on Mars. Apparently, all the kids were still in school.

Just as I was about to give up and run back to Nana's air conditioner, something amazing happened. My body began to feel light. My stomach stopped growling. The scalding air felt *good*, like a cedar-lined sauna. Purification via perspiration. It baked my insides and quieted the anxiety hum in my brain. I felt relaxed, released. Oddly, the hideous turn my life had taken was now a fuzzy *ping* in the back of my brain instead of a throbbing ping-pong from the left side of my head to the right. My lungs acclimated to the desert heat and felt soothed instead of scorched. I inhaled deeply and enjoyed the crackle of my nose hairs as they fried. In spite of myself, I began to feel lighthearted. Hopeful, even. Miraculously, I found myself thinking, Maybe everything will be okay.

"Probably sunstroke," I joked to myself. Then I stopped, took a deep breath, and felt my chest expand with warmth. Yeah, I could handle visiting my grandmother here once or twice a year. It wouldn't be so bad. Even if she was bonkers.

In the distance, I heard voices and splashing in the pool. Hey, there *was* life on Mars!

"Myrna looks like a Siamese cat."

As I snuck up to the chain-link fence surrounding the pool area, I heard female voices and the *blap, blap* of gentle swimming.

"Her ears wiggle when she blinks, he pulled so tight."

Juan Dog and I crouched behind a prickly, dry bush. The voices woke him. His ears were sticking straight up.

"She told me she wanted to look younger than her ex's new wife."

An old lady on a sagging raft in the shallow end of the pool had a thatched hut on top of her head. I'd never seen such a huge hat. Her geriatric friend was painting her toenails under an umbrella near the diving board. They shouted sentences at each other across the pool.

"Her mouth looks like the joker in that movie. What was it? *Batman*?"

Both women wore brightly flowered, skirted swimsuits. Their legs resembled blue cheese, and it was obvious they had to bend way over to pour their pendulous breasts into their suits' pointed double-D cups.

"Myrna's eyebrows are over her ears! Little earmuffs!" One

of the antique bathing beauties laughed so hard she erupted in a coughing fit.

Yip! Yip!

"Shhh," I whispered into Juan's big ear.

Licking his tiny lips, he leaped out of my arms and wiggled his little body through the gate. Apparently, Juan now associated old women with delicious food.

Yip! Yip!

"Juan! Get over here!"

"What on earth?" The lady with the red toenails hoisted herself out of the chaise longue and waddled over to the fence on her heels.

"Juan Dog! Come!" I said through gritted teeth, still huddled behind the bush.

Yippy. Yip.

"What a darling puppy!" The woman with the toenails bent down to pick Juan Dog up. "Look, Charlotte," she called to the old lady on the raft, "remember the Taco Bell puppy!"

Juan hated being called a puppy, *especially* the Taco Bell puppy. I emerged from behind the bush and entered through the gate. "You little rascal," I said reprimandingly, reaching up to save him. But the lady held on.

"He doesn't like strangers," I said. Mocking me, Juan gently licked the lady's cheek and tucked his little head into her triple chins.

"There, there," she cooed. "I'm not a stranger."

"I'm just visiting," I stammered. "I should get back."

Charlotte and the old lady exchanged a look. "Oh, we know who you are."

"You know me?" I blinked.

"We've been expecting you! Elizabeth's granddaughter, right?"

Elizabeth? Was it possible I was named after my grandmother and no one bothered to mention it?

"You're one of the Madrigal kids, right?"

Of course it was possible. Anything was possible with my family's don't-ask-don't-tell policy. Geez, I'd only learned my very own grandmother was alive and kicking an hour ago.

"Um, right," I said.

Charlotte, the raft lady shouted, "Do you have a swimsuit on under those shorts, hon?"

Charlotte slid off her raft and plopped onto the pool stairs. Clutching the railing, she heaved herself up, padding along the hot cement to fetch her towel. Her feet looked like dried starfish. Suddenly, the Ping-Pong game in my head resumed. I wanted to go home. I longed for Geometry class and our dirt backyard. What was Nadine doing now? Had she forgotten me already?

Annoyed at my parents all over again for ruining my life, I reached for Juan. The old woman held him closer.

"Could you please give me my dog back?"

"He's so comfy!" The woman holding Juan turned and lowered herself onto her chaise with Juan still lost in the folds of her skin. The other one hobbled closer to me, leaned forward almost touching my nose with her nose. "Yep. I see the resemblance," she said. "You've got a lot of Elizabeth in you. Let me get you a bathing suit. I have an extra one in my locker."

Still dripping, she turned and hobbled off.

"I can't stay," I called after her. "As soon as I get my dog, I'm leaving."

Scoffing, she said over her shoulder, "Don't worry. I just had the bathing suit cleaned." Then she added, "By the way, I'm Charlotte and Dr. Doolittle over there is Mim."

Mim was busy tickling Juan under the chin. I'd never seen him so happy.

"Nice to meet you both," I said stiffly. "But, uh, my family is probably looking for me."

Mim said, "Leave the Taco Bell puppy with us. He's falling asleep."

Juan Dog's eyes were droopy and I could swear I saw his lips curved upward in a sappy grin. Traitor.

"I can't. We're moving into a new house and—"

"It's okay. I'll bring him over later, when he wakes up." Mim was now rocking Juan back and forth. Was that *snoring* I heard?

"We're neighbors," Mim added. "I live on Eden Way and Charlotte's on Nirvana." She kissed the top of Juan's head. "You're on Valhalla Drive, right?"

"No. My grandmother lives on Paradise Way."

"I mean *your* trailer is on Valhalla Drive."

"We don't have a trailer," I said.

"It's not ready yet?" asked Charlotte. "Your granny has been driving the construction workers crazy."

I started to feel sick. Please, God, let heatstroke distort your hearing. And, if it does, please, God, let me have heatstroke.

"*Mobile home*, Charlotte," Mim said. "You don't want this sweet young girl thinking she's moving into a trailer."

Now, I began to feel faint. Juan continued to snore blissfully.

Mim asked me, "Did your grandmother tell you about the big party?"

My inner Ping-Pong game was suddenly an Olympic event in my head with slam serves and killer volleys.

"The whole trailer park is invited to your trailer warming. Mim is bringing her famous baked beans, I'm making cake—"

In a blur of sound waves, I lurched forward and snatched Juan Dog from the folds of Mim's neck. Startled, he woke up and shook his head. Together, we bolted for the gate, Juan's huge ears flapping.

"No running around the pool!" Charlotte shouted. "Sunset Park rules!"

chapter fourteen

"How could you?!" I burst through Nana's trailer's door.

Mom's head snapped up, a half-eaten noodle whipping her face.

"There you are!" Nana said. "Your lunch is still warm, Libby. Would you like milk? A soda of some kind?"

"Were you ever going to tell us? Did you think we wouldn't notice?" I practically spat the question at my mother.

"Libby, Nana made wild pig spaghetti! From *scratch*." Elated, Dirk dragged a piece of warm garlic bread through the sauce at the bottom of his pasta bowl.

"Wild *boar* fettuccine," Nana corrected him, "with truffle oil."

"You're not going to want to eat when I tell you what's going on," I said to my brothers. "We're moving *here*. Into this trailer park! Not a house. A *trailer*."

"Mobile home," Dirk said, then he gazed lovingly at his grandmother. Nana smiled and stroked his head. Then she glanced at Mom, but Mom just stared at her fork and licked wild boar off her lips.

"You're wrong, Libby," Rif said calmly.

"I'm not wrong!" I exploded. "Am I, Mom?"

My mother gulped. Juan Dog bounded out of my arms and sat, shaking, at my mother's feet, hoping for a spill.

"Not all mobile homes are big kitchens, you know," Nana said gently.

"I can't live in a trailer park!" I cried. "Only losers live in trailer parks! Our house in Chatsworth was bad enough! Who ever dreamed we could sink lower than that?"

It was hurtful to my grandmother, I knew. But I was too upset to care. Did she care that my parents had ruined my life?

"No," said Rif. "You're wrong about me not wanting to eat. This food rocks. No matter where we live."

All I could do was stare. What was *wrong* with these people? Was *everyone* in my family completely around the bend?

Mom finally chose to speak. "Eat something, Libby. You'll feel better."

My body nearly levitated off the floor, I was so angry. "That's your solution to the end of my life? Eat a wild pig?"

"Boar," Mom said quietly.

What could I say? I was, literally, speechless. I felt like howling. How could this be happening? I'd never have a boyfriend now! My serious kiss was seriously gone — lost among the septic tanks and Astro Turf lawns.

Too upset to formulate actual words, I stamped my foot, crossed my arms in front of my chest, tried to mentally block the amazing aroma from entering my nose, and shot Mom a death stare.

"I have a fabulous idea!" Nana clapped her hands together. Her rings sounded like a pocket full of change. "Let's not wait for Lance. Let's look at your new home right now."

Dirk squealed. "Will I have my own room?"

"Absolutely! You each have your own room."

Good, I thought. I can't wait to lock myself in mine.

"Come." Nana held her hand out to me. Dirk reached up and slipped his grubby hand into hers.

"I like it here," he said, beaming up at her.

"You'll all love it here, just as I do. Follow me."

Love living in a trailer park? Never. No way. Not *ever.* No matter how much I was dying to taste wild boar.

Everybody scraped their chairs back and stood. But instead of leaving out the front door, Nana led us to the back of her trailer. We wound around her dining room table and snaked past her toilet armoire.

Lagging behind the others, Rif said to me, "Don't you know that it doesn't matter where you live? Life sucks everywhere."

Finally, someone in my family made sense.

Just beyond Nana's back door, there was a tiny backyard, with one chair and a round red Weber barbecue. The heat instantly calmed me. I felt less like exploding, more like pulling a sheet over my head and willing myself into a coma.

"This is where I sunbathe," Nana said.

What a hideous view for her poor neighbors, I thought.

It was still dead quiet except for the humming air conditioners. A low, chain-link fence with a tiny, swinging gate separated two trailer lots. Nana held the gate open for us and shuffled us through.

"Should we be trespassing through someone else's backyard?" Mom asked.

"You're not trespassing, Dot," Nana said. "You're home."

"Home?"

"Home?"

"Home?!" An echo passed through our family. Dirk's jaw hung open as he grinned; Juan stepped aside to avoid the inevitable splat of drool. I felt my whole body melt into the ground. My mother looked dumbfounded. Clearly, she was shocked to hear that we would be living right behind my father's mother. I mean, if you shouted out the rear window of Nana's mobile home, you'd hear it clear as day at our place. Nana's suntanning sessions would now be *our* scenery. Suddenly, I found my voice.

"Eat something, Mom," I said sarcastically. "You'll feel better."

Mom didn't even snarl at me; she was too dazed.

"C'mon inside!" Nana was positively glowing. "I've been running the air conditioner!"

Inside, Nana swept her arms open like she was Vanna White. "This is the living room," she sang. "Over there is the bathroom. Full size! A tub, even. The master bedroom is in the back, and, just as I said, you each have your own rooms!" Nana's eyes were bright white elevator buttons, her smile psychotic.

"Where's the kitchen?" Mom asked innocently.

"At my place!" My grandmother exploded in glee. "That's the beauty of it! I gutted the whole trailer and redid it for you! I figured you needed bedrooms more than a kitchen so I got rid of all the appliances. Of course, I bought you a hot plate. . . ." She pointed to the corner of the living room. "You know, in case you want a cup of tea in the middle of the night. Isn't it fabulous!? I've already called my editor friend at *Trailer Life* and he's sending over a photographer as soon as you get settled in. Isn't it just the most fabulous thing?!"

Again, nobody moved. Beads of sweat appeared on Mom's upper lip even though the air conditioner was on full blast. Her face was flushed. Now I felt scared. As soon as Dad finished running his *errands* (yeah, right), he'd stumble into this new home and discover it had no heart. Not only that, but the woman he'd rather mourn than talk to was only smelling distance away. Dad was going to freak out. Could you bash a hole in a metal wall?

"See, honey?" Nana said to me, wrapping both arms around my shoulders. "Everything's going to be just fine."

Her hug smelled of garlic. I stood as stiff as a garden gnome.

"That's what you think, because you don't have a clue."

That's what I *wanted* to say. Instead, I said nothing. My stomach was doing cartwheels; the Ping-Pong match in my head was into overtime. All I kept thinking was, How unfair is it that my life is over when it was just starting to begin?

At that moment, we heard the squeak of Dad's U-Move brakes as he pulled up to the front door of our brand-new kitchenless mobile home.

"Is that Lance?" Nana asked excitedly, letting go of me.

My heart started doing cartwheels, too. Rif disappeared down the hall and Dirk's face got all pinched like he was about to cry.

"You'd better go," Mom said quickly to Nana. "I mean"—she softened her tone—"we should get settled in."

The truck door slammed as Mom gently prodded Nana toward the back door before Dad came in through the front.

"I haven't seen my son in so long I don't even know if I'll recognize him," Nana said.

Now Mom draped her arm around Nana's shoulder. "We need to give him a few minutes to relax before the big family reunion. You know how it is after a long drive."

Nana obviously didn't know how it was, but she was too smart to question it. Either that or the fact that my mother was practically shoving her out the back door was enough of a hint. She dutifully made her exit, waved at Dirk and me, and sailed off in a flapping triangle of material, announcing over her shoulder, "Dinner's at seven sharp. I'm making mulligatawny!"

Mom greeted Dad at the door like she was Donna Reed on speed. "Hi, honey!" she sang. "You made it! Come in! Come in! Come in!"

My brother and I cowered in the corner of our new empty living room. Dad growled, "I got lost." The moment he entered our new pad, we knew he hadn't been lost at all. His breath smelled sour and yeasty. His glasses were about to fall off his nose completely.

"So this is it?" he asked.

"It certainly is! Look how spacious!" Mom was whacked out. Her hands fluttered midair like they were trying to escape her wrists. I watched them flop, left then right, like some ghoulish tennis match.

"Where's the woman?" Dad asked.

"She's invited us for dinner!" Mom squealed. Dad groaned. Now my mother's hands clapped insanely together. "Don't worry, we have plenty of time to unpack."

With that, Mom turned to us and flapped her hands toward the door. I took it to mean that she wanted the caravan from the U-Move to the trailer to begin. It was too surreal to question. Still upset, I yelled down the hall for Rif. He appeared, reeking of smoke, and walked outside to the open U-Move truck. Reluctantly, I followed.

"Libby, grab the other end of the coffee table, would you?"

"Rif, kiss my ass, would you?"

My parents got us into this mess, they could move us into it, too. No way was I lifting a thing. I just stood there, arms crossed in front of my chest.

"Libby!" Mom appeared, looking frantic. Dad was inside. "Forget the table," she whispered. "Find the coffee and the coffee-pot as soon as you can. We've got to sober your father up before dinner."

It took my father about twenty minutes to realize there was no kitchen. The coffeepot percolated in a corner of the living room floor. Mom snatched all the boxes labeled "dishes" or "pots and pans" and quietly stacked them near the hot plate. My brothers and I walked back and forth from the U-Move like robots, waiting for the fuse to blow. It wasn't until Dad and Rif rolled the refrigerator through the trailer door on a dolly that the fireworks began.

"I'll take it from here, Dad," Rif said once they were inside. I admired the effort and wondered where Rif planned to stow the fridge.

Dad said, "You can't handle this baby yourself." Then he yanked his baggy old work jeans up at the waist, tilted the dolly unsteadily back, and began to roll. Dirk, my mother, and I just stood there and stared, openmouthed, like three Pez dispensers. Dad stopped, scrunched his eyebrows together, and said, "Hey, wait a minute."

That's when Mom decided she had to go to the bathroom. *Chicken.*

Dad turned to me and asked, "Where the hell is the kitchen?"

"Interesting you should ask," I said, stalling, waiting for the toilet to flush and Mom to reappear. But the only sound was the *fwonk!* of the refrigerator as Dad set it back on the ground.

"What the . . . Dot! Get out here."

Now I heard the toilet flush.

"Coffee, Dad? I made it fresh." I pointed to the coffeemaker on the floor, but that just made him madder.

"*Now*, Dot."

My mother reappeared in the living room with fresh lipstick and a pained expression. She said, "Yes?" all innocent, like she didn't know what was about to go down.

"I was wondering, dear, if you could lead the way into the kitchen. It's so hard to see from behind the refrigerator." Dad didn't seem drunk at all now. In fact, he seemed more than sober.

"We all have our own rooms," Dirk said, extremely close to tears.

Mom took a deep breath. "Don't get mad, Lot," she began.

"Mad? Why should I be mad? Has someone *stolen* our

kitchen? Did someone sell it? You were in charge of arranging this whole move. Surely you wouldn't forget to make sure we had a kitchen, would you? Not when the kitchen is your favorite room in the house."

Here we go.

Mom bit her lip, tears began to rise in her eyes. "Your mother—" she started.

"My mother? What about my mother? Didn't I tell you that I would only agree to this move if my mother was a minimal part of our lives? If I rarely had to see her or talk to her or even hear about her? Didn't I?"

"Yes," Mom said softly.

"So why am I hearing her name before I've even moved into my house?"

Uh-oh. I glanced at the back window. His mother was probably hearing this entire conversation.

"Your mother had the trailer redone," Mom said quietly.

"Redone?"

"Without a kitchen."

"What?!"

"Dad, we all have our own rooms!" Dirk burst into tears.

This time Dad shouted, "Then why don't you all *go* to your own rooms!"

Like fighter pilots at an air show, we peeled off in unison. Snatching Juan Dog, I chose the bedroom at the far end of the trailer, Dirk ran into the room next to mine, and Rif shut the door of the third bedroom, lit a cigarette, and blew the smoke out his small, slide window. I could smell it right away. If Dirk was doing what I was doing, we both had our ears pressed to the door.

"You *trusted* that woman?!" My father shrieked. "It's bad enough we had to lower ourselves to move into a trailer my mother bought—"

"Mobile home."

"Look around, Dot! Do you see any *wheels* on this thing? They only call them mobile homes so you can fool yourself into thinking you haven't sunk this low permanently!"

"Keep your voice down, Lot. She'll hear you."

"Hear me? Where is she? Hiding in the closet with her broom?"

"Shhhh, Lot. She's next door."

"Next door?" My father sounded like his head was about to pop. "My mother is next *door*? What kind of dumb-assed, pea-brained, simpleminded, stupid—"

"STOP!" Mom erupted in a bloodcurdling scream.

Even Juan stopped fidgeting. I think the whole trailer park must have halted, perched in mid-sentence waiting to hear what would happen next. My heart pounded out of my chest. I couldn't move, couldn't breathe.

"Stop it! Stop it! Stop it! Stop it!"

Mom screamed again, then she got deathly quiet, and Dad didn't say anything more. The silence in the mobile home was as thick as tapioca.

"You've come to the end of the line, Lot." My mother's voice scared me. It was as sharp and ragged as a hangnail. "With me, your children, your life as you've been living it. The end of the line."

Dad mumbled something I couldn't hear. Something indignant. Mom barreled on through.

"It's not *my* fault we're in this mess. You should be grateful your mother took us in."

"Grateful? The woman hasn't spoken to her only son in twenty years!"

"Give me a break! You haven't spoken to *her*."

"Why should I? Where does she get off telling me I can't have a beer?"

Now it sounded as though my mother's head would pop.

"Can't have a beer? Can you even hear yourself? Your father drank himself to death and your mother had every right to refuse to watch the same thing happen to her son. All she said was she'd talk to you when you stopped drinking. *You* let twenty years pass!"

Oh my God. So *that* was the big "family" sort of fight! At first, I couldn't believe my ears. My father kept a grandmother out of our lives because he'd rather have a beer? He preferred to pretend his own mother was *dead* than give up the brew? Then I realized it was *exactly* like my dad. Hadn't he once forgotten to pick me up at school when I was sick because he went to El Torito for lunch and had three tequila shooters? Didn't I spend four hours doubled over on the nurse's cot watching her feel sorry for me?

Yeah, I could imagine my dad being so selfish. I mean, we were living in a trailer! What further evidence did I need?

When Mom continued, her voice was slow and icy. "You put me in charge, and I *took* charge, Lot. Are you ready for this?"

Dad didn't say a word. I still couldn't breathe, couldn't move. My mom didn't sound like my mom at all when she said, "I made a deal with your mother. We can live here as long as you don't drink. Your mother has given us a roof over our heads and a chance to start over. Fall off the wagon and we're out of here. *Homeless.* Your family, Lot, will be out on the street because of you. Your drinking cost you your job, your home, your friends. Keep it up and it will cost you your family, too. You've said a million times you can stop drinking whenever you want to. Now's the time to prove it. You say you're not an alcoholic; fine, it shouldn't be a problem. If it is, get help. We have no money and nowhere else to go. It's up to you now. *Only* you."

The mobile home suddenly vibrated with the *thump, thump, thump* of my mother's footsteps down the hall. I nearly jumped through the ceiling when she knocked on my door.

"Let's go, kids," she said, pounding on all three of our bedroom doors. "Time to get you registered for school."

That's when the doorbell rang.

"Get lost!" Dad shouted.

A tiny voice on the other side of our new metal front door squeaked, "I'm from *Trailer Life.* I'm here to photograph your mobile home."

chapter Fifteen

Desert Valley High School was a disaster area. Cracked asphalt, peeling paint, tired old cinder-block buildings that looked more like bunkers than classrooms. Everything was litter-box gray or dirt brown, even the grass, the trees, and the distant Calico Mountains.

Getting there was even worse.

"There's just so much I can take," Mom muttered to herself, the car leaping forward at green lights, jerking to a stop at reds. "He thinks he can ruin my life? I don't *thinkywink* so."

An open bag of Doritos sat between my mom's legs. Her fingers were stained orange. We'd been driving around in circles for half an hour, past the same tiny taco stand, muffler repair shop, dentist's office, insurance storefront. Nobody said a word. Except Mom, of course, who talked mostly to herself in angry, guttural grunts.

"I'm at the end of my rope. It's about time he was at the end of his."

Finally, she looked right and left out the windshield and sighed. "Rif, will you please get the map out of the glove box? That school is *somewhere* around here."

While Rif rummaged around, Mom kept circling. Past the tiny taco stand, the muffler repair shop, dentist's office, insurance storefront. Sitting in the backseat, with Juan Dog on my lap, I watched Barstow pass by the window yet again. It never looked any better. I felt so many emotions—sad, scared, angry, upset—it was impossible to fully wallow in just one. Well, there was one feeling that rose above all the rest: confusion. Complete mind-numbing confusion. A mere week ago, I was struggling with Geometry, memorizing the back of Zack Nash's neck. Now my life was spun around and plopped on its head, totally disoriented. It took all the strength I had just to keep my eyes open and focused so I could see the bad news coming and dodge it before it hit me, *splat*, right in the face.

"This is a map of *California*, Mom," Rif said. "I can get you to San Diego or Sacramento."

"How hard could it be to find a high school?" Mom circled Barstow one more time. Suddenly, Dirk leaned forward from the backseat and blurted out, "Is Dad an alcoholic?"

I held my breath. Juan did, too. We leaned forward with Dirk, listened to the hum of the engine and the soft blowing of the air conditioner. My brothers and I looked like an exhibit in the wax museum, waiting, locked in anticipation. I felt thrilled and terrified at the same time. The palms of my hands tingled. I'd been waiting for this moment all my life. A moment of truth. No more hiding. No more secrets. The other shoe could finally drop. My family would finally face what we'd secretly known for so long.

Mom took a deep breath, licked her fingers clean. We braced our-selves.

"There it is!" she cried. "Desert Valley High. I should have stayed on the road I was on before!"

I groaned. Story of my life.

I felt tears well up again, felt my chest pinch. Desert Valley High made Fernando High look like a Hawaiian postcard. WISH YOU WERE HERE. Wish I was *there*.

Mom parked right in front of the front steps. Wouldn't you know it, we got there exactly at three o'clock, just as the metal double doors were spitting out students. She stopped too sud-denly and the car lurched and screeched, causing everybody to look at us.

"Oops," she said. "My heel caught."

"Don't stop here!" I shrieked, sinking low in the seat, pulling my sunglasses out of my pack and slipping them on my red, puffy face. Now my main emotion was complete and utter mortifica-tion.

"Mom! There's a parking lot!"

Ignoring me, she said, "I'll only be a few minutes." Then she heaved herself out of the car, tugged at her too-tight lime green dress, and took the car keys with her. I wanted to shrivel up and tuck myself into my own crumpled Kleenex. Better still, I wanted to disappear altogether.

"Nice car, man." Some students walked past us, looked at Rif, and laughed. Rif reached into his hair for a cigarette.

"Do you think they have a pool?" Dirk asked. Rif and I both rolled our eyes. A pool? This high school looked like it didn't even have a cafeteria. While Fernando High was all spread out, my new school seemed like it had fallen into a trash compactor. There were a lot of kids, but they were squished among the tired old buildings.

My heart sank. How could this happen? How could life keep getting *worse*? My spirit felt like a marble in a fishbowl, sinking quickly and permanently to the bottom. Peeking out the car window, I observed my future classmates in their natural habitat. Most looked like thugs to me. Tough no-smilers. Girls with thick black hair and even thicker black eyeliner. Boys with buzz cuts and tattoos and way-too-baggy pants. Very scary. What terrified me most, though, was the incredible amount of skin. Yeah, it was hot out, but man! The girls wore short shorts with platform slides and spaghetti-strap T-shirts with no bra. They clipped their long hair up in messy twists and laughed and chatted as if there wasn't less than a skimpy yard of fabric between their naked bodies and the whole wide world. Two different couples were all knotted up, making out right there on the front steps. In front of *everybody*. As I sat there, the car getting hotter and hotter, it felt like I was stalled on the railroad track—nothing to do but hope the white puff of smoke in the distance isn't the locomotive.

"Look, Libby, I found Waldo." Dirk pointed to some nerd in a red-and-white-striped T-shirt sitting on a retaining wall, reading a book called *Calculus and You*.

"Now maybe you'll finally have a boyfriend." Snorting as he laughed, Dirk sounded just like a wild boar.

"Waldo" didn't look half bad. At least he didn't scare me to death.

By now, tons of students had swarmed around the car, checking us out. Some pointed through the window, others indicated there was fresh meat in their midst by flicking their heads in our direction. It was so hot, sweat marks were expanding in my armpits. My sunglasses slid down the damp bridge of my nose.

Through a clenched jaw I declared, "I'm not going here. I'll live with Nadine. I'll join the circus."

It got harder and harder to breathe inside the car. We didn't dare roll down the windows, clinging to last bit of air-conditioned air. Just as I was on the verge of hyperventilating, Rif startled me out of my impending panic attack by opening the car door and stepping out. Dirk, wiping his nose on his sleeve, followed him.

"Where are you going?!" I screeched. Neither one of them paid any attention to me. Typical! They got out of the car and let the crowd swallow them up. Calm as you please. Rif glanced right and left and lit up. Can you believe it? Just like that. Rif was Rif no matter where he was or who happened to be with him. And Dirk, well Dirk basically imitated everything his older brother did without thinking too much about it. Which left me, the emotional psycho.

Soon it was clear I'd suffocate if I stayed in the airless car much longer. No way was I going to sit there and fry alone. I swung open the door and squirmed out of the backseat. "Stay," I commanded Juan Dog. But it was so hot and he hung his head so pathetically I relented.

"Oh, all right." I picked him up, slammed the car door shut, and scrambled after Rif and Dirk across the school parking lot to the edge of a brown football field. Breathless, I commanded, "Rif, get back in the car." But even as I said it, I knew he'd scoff at me. Which he did. Dirk, the idiot, stuck his tongue out and shoved his hands deep into his pockets, trying to look cool.

"Rif . . ." I said again. This time I tapped my foot. That ought to do it.

"Get lost," Rif said to me. Then he walked away and merged into a nearby group of lowlifes. Dirk joined him.

"You new?" one of the guys asked Rif.

"Will be," said Rif, taking another deep puff before stamping out his cigarette.

"Cool, man."

"Hope so."

"What year?"

"Junior."

"Whoa, dude."

Their Neanderthal sentences drove me crazy. I spun on my heels and loudly stomped back to the car.

"Your girlfriend?" I heard one of them ask.

"My *sister.*"

"Oh, man."

"No kidding."

Mom still hadn't returned. Right back? Yeah, right! Juan was panting and I was sweating so much my hair was plastered to my forehead. Everyone was looking at me, talking behind their hands. I hurried to the car, got in, and sat there like a blob of bread dough in the oven.

"The girl and the mutt are two hot tamales," I heard somebody say. Then I heard lots of somebodies laugh. Totally red-faced, I rolled down the window, but it was no use. The air was so stifling, Juan and I had to get out of the car before we both passed out.

"Oooo, how *cute*."

I froze.

"Look, Sylvana, the Taco Bell dog!"

Oh, God.

Before I could turn around, a swarm was upon me. There must have been only three or four girls, but it felt like hundreds. Juan Dog and I were instantly swallowed up in CK cologne, lip gloss, squeals, and skin. Lots of skin.

"He's so cute."

"Look at the darling puppy!"

"Can I hold him?"

"Number *one*, he's *not* a puppy. He hates being called a puppy. It's not his fault that he's so small. Do you call short people little babies? No? I didn't think so. Number *two*, we bought him *years* before that stupid Taco Bell commercial. He's *not* the Taco Bell dog. He's *Juan* Dog, a beautiful canine in his own right. Number *three*, my mother will be here any moment and we have to get going, back to our very complete lives, away from this dust bowl dump. So in answer to your question, no, you can't hold him. He's mine and he hates girls named Sylvana who have long, straight hair and tan legs and flat belly buttons with gold hoops sticking out of them."

That's what I *wanted* to say.

Instead I said, "Yeah. Okay." Then I just stood there. Like a dope. I let them pass Juan from one set of pastel-painted finger-nails to another like he was some kind of hairy, shivering football or something. That's what I did, feeling as small and ashamed as I'm sure Juan did.

"Can I let him run around a little?" one of the Sylvanas asked.

"Well . . ."

She set his tiny paws on a patch of hot, prickly, dead grass and he hopped around pitifully.

"How *cute!*"

Before I could bend down to save him, Juan hunched up his back, brought his hind legs up close to his front legs, and squeezed one off. In front of God and the Sylvanas and all of D.V. High, Juan Dog *pooped.*

"Oh," one of the girls covered her white teeth and tittered.

"Eeewwww," said another.

Beet faced, I lamely asked, "Anyone have a Baggie?"

They looked confused, like I wanted to take it home or something. "Or a tissue, scrap of paper, gum wrapper, anything?" My voice was growing weak.

Nobody said a word. They stared at me as if I'd ruined the party. Juan beamed. Yeah, *he* was feeling fine.

"This your car, ma'am?"

Wheeling around, I saw a police officer standing at the front of our car. In his mirrored sunglasses I could see my tiny purple-red face.

"Uh . . . no . . . it's . . . uh, my mom's." The flashing lights on top of his squad car had attracted the attention of the whole school. What, he was going to arrest me? Wasn't the Robo-Cop routine a tad over the top? I wanted to die.

"You can't park here," he said. "The school buses pull in here."

"Oh. Well . . . my mom . . ."

"Let's go," Sylvana said to her friends. The other Sylvanas nodded and stepped over Juan's poop, away from me as fast as possible.

"You going to clean that up?" the officer asked me, pointing to the little Tootsie Rolls Juan left on the grass. We were now encircled by a growing crowd of silent, gaping students. I looked up and saw Waldo with his calculus book under one arm and a superior smirk on his face.

Lord, please take me now.

"Bethy?"

Her voice pierced the crowd, panicked and shrill. "Bethy?!" The students receded like low tide and made way for my mom. Fingers splayed, her tight green dress wrinkled, her baby toe poking out of her high-heeled sandals, Mom rushed forward, her face flushed with worry. "What happened?"

"Nothing, Mom, we —" Before I could say more, she took one more fatal step and landed smack dab on the center of Juan Dog's *poopadilly.*

"Eeewwwww." The crowd groaned in unison. Turning my head away, I silently prayed for a quick, massive heart attack to put me out of my misery.

"What on earth?" Mom looked down. "Oh, Bethy!"

"Oh, Bethy!" Someone in the crowd loudly mimicked her. It was Rif.

Not the type of coronary from which you can be revived, please, but instant, permanent, chest-clutching death.

"Move along, kids. Party's over." The cop sidestepped the poop pancake and dispersed the crowd. Someone joked, "Ah, don't be a party pooper!" and everyone howled. Mom slipped her shoe off and scraped it on the curb while Juan toddled up the hill with the group.

"Juan! Get back here, you little runt!" Juan, looking scared, ignored my mom and quickened his pace. "Bethy, go get him."

"Rif, go get him!" I said.

"Dirk, go get the dog."

Dirk, low man on the Madrigal totem pole, skulked up the hill to get Juan, who had stuck his head inside somebody's lunch bag.

"Where are your keys, Mom?" All I wanted to do was crawl into the backseat, turn on the air conditioner, and stay there till college.

"Will you at least give me a Kleenex?" Her smelly sandal dangled from one chubby finger.

"Here." Rif appeared out of nowhere with a fresh tissue in his hand. Prince Charming.

"Thank you," Mom said to Rif, sneering at me.

What did I do?

"Your *keys*, Mom?"

"Your dog, miss?" An unfamiliar voice spoke behind me. Turning, I was suddenly face-to-face with the most gorgeous creature I'd ever seen. Okay, scratch that. He wasn't Brad or Leo or Zack Nash. He wasn't drop-dead dazzling in a traditional Hollywood hunk way. This guy was *deep*, soulful. I could tell. He wore glasses, though they were the way cool kind. His T-shirt was untucked, his baggy shorts well-pressed, his Top-Siders brand-new. This guy had blond hair and pearly-white fingernails and firm ancillary veins that snaked all the way up his naturally muscled arms.

This was a guy I could definitely seriously kiss.

"Miss?"

"Eliza*beth*." Mom's impatient voice felt like a toothpick in my ear.

"What?"

"Take the *dog*."

Oh. I suddenly became aware that the guy was holding Juan Dog out to me. Juan's little legs were wiggling frantically, his neck strained. He looked like a cockroach flipped on its back.

"Oh! Sorry." I came to, blushing instantly, grabbing my dog. "This is Juan." *Great, Libby, introduce your dog!*

"I found him in my lunch sack," the guy said. "Apparently Juan likes leftover meat loaf sandwiches more than I do."

I laughed way too loud and long for the joke.

"Elizabeth, take the damn dog, get your brothers, and get in the car."

Mortified, I stammered an awkward "thank you" and glared at my mother as I struggled to slither gracefully under the seatbelt strap, into the backseat of our crappy old car. Let *her* get my brothers, I thought. What, I'm their babysitter?

As soon as I was settled in, I looked out the window to watch the boy who just replaced Zack Nash in my dreams, a serious candidate for my serious kiss. But he was already gone. I sighed. Juan sighed, too, curled up on my lap, and licked his lips. To my utter amazement, I found myself thinking maybe Barstow wasn't going to be so bad after all.

chapter sixteen

"Lance!"

Dressed in a fresh caftan, this one a blinding chartreuse, Nana completely encircled my father in fabric. Tears streamed down her wrinkled brown cheeks.

"My baby boy, Lance!"

I held my breath, braced for another explosion. Dad simply said, "Mother." Then he busted free from her embrace.

"Let me look at you," Nana squealed, fluttering after him.

Mom, pale with panic, lunged for the table in the center of Nana's trailer kitchen. "Something smells scrumptious! Shall we sit anywhere?"

"You look tired," Nana said to my dad. "It's been rough, hasn't it?"

"Rif, you sit there. Libby, sit there . . ."

Nobody moved. We stared slack jawed at my dad and his mom. Nana kept pawing him; he kept inching backward. Dad was nearly pressed against the toilet armoire when Nana said, "I'm so proud of you, son. How long have you been sober?"

"How 'bout I sit *here* and, Dirk, you sit *there*?" Mom's voice screeched like a long skid. She flashed us a black look that said Sit. Down. *Now.*

We sat.

Dad said nothing, skirted past his mother, and took a seat at the far end of the large table.

"All that matters is we're here now, right, Lance? The whole family." Nana smeared the last of her tears across her face with the back of her hand.

"Lot," Dad muttered, reaching for one of the steaming, aromatic tureens in the center of the table.

"Yes." Nana sniffed. "There's plenty for everyone."

"My name is *Lot* now," said Dad. "Lance died twenty years ago."

Dinner that night was so tense it nearly snapped. My parents weren't speaking to each other, we didn't dare say a word, and my grandmother was oblivious to the fact that her newfound family was on the verge of a meltdown.

"Everybody unpacked?" she chirped.

Dad guzzled colas all during dinner. He flung his head back, opened his mouth, and poured the carbonated sugar directly down his throat.

"That can't be good for you, Lance," his mother said.

Dad responded with a deep, round, gaseous belch.

"It doesn't matter," Nana said. Then she repeated, for like the millionth time, "I'm just so happy to finally have you home."

Puppy eyed, she stood and reached across the table to squeeze his hand. He snatched it away.

My emotional Richter scale had already registered a megaquake and several aftershocks that day. By dinnertime, I was wiped out. I didn't feel much of anything. Except hunger.

Gastronomically, my grandmother was awesome. Her food danced down my tongue, exciting each bud on its way to my throat. The first bite was a burst of intense flavor, then subtle layers of smoke, spice, sweet, and salt erupted like tiny fireworks. It terrified me. I was dying to pile my plate high with curried eggplant, grilled lamb shanks, and fresh spinach bread with herb butter. Not to mention mulligatawny soup. The rich colors on her table were as luscious as the rich smells. Every meal here? I was never going to make it. It was one thing to eat a Grilled Chicken Salad at McDonald's when my family was devouring Double Quarter Pounders with Cheese. I could handle refusing to eat seven hundred and sixty calories and forty-eight fat grams of fast food. But gourmet food? Controlling my portion sizes was going to be next to impossible.

"More mulligatawny, Libby?" Nana asked.

I swallowed hard. "No, thanks."

"It's one of Emeril's recipes," she said. I stared blankly, as did my whole family. "'Bam? Crank it up a notch?'"

Nothing. Nana glanced up at the heavens, made a praying gesture with her hands. "Thank you, God, for bringing my family to me so I can teach them about *life!*" Looking at the rest of my family, she asked, "Who's ready for more soup?"

Mom and Rif held their bowls up; Dad gulped another cola. Dirk said, "I've never eaten yellow soup before. It's so good I don't want to know what's in it!"

Nana glanced at God once more.

"Can I please have more yellow rice, too?" Dirk asked.

While Nana served us, she asked, "Who knows why saffron is the most expensive spice in the world?"

Yip!

"Anyone?"

Juan, sitting beneath the table at my feet, was impatient for me to drop another chunk of lamb.

"Because," she said, "the orange stigmas of the saffron plant have to be picked by hand."

No one responded. Juan Dog licked the Italian tile floor.

"Can you imagine? By *hand*!"

Mom smiled a crack and nodded her head. Dad took another gulp. I noticed his hands were shaking and his forehead was damp.

"Who knows what *poha* means?"

Dirk erupted in giggles.

"Dirk? You've studied Indian cooking?"

Still laughing Dirk said, "No, but Juan *pohaed* in your backyard earlier!"

Peeved, I scowled at him. He wasn't supposed to tell! I didn't have a Baggie with me and it was still sitting there. Oblivious, Nana barreled on through.

"*Poha* is rice!" she said. "*Aloo* is a potato, *kishmish* are raisins, *podina* is mint. These are all common ingredients in the Indian kitchen."

Mom mumbled something about the food being delicious no matter what was in it. Dad kept his head down and chewed.

145

"It takes a while to familiarize yourself with all the terms." Nana seemed so unaware of the tension around her table it occurred to me she might be senile. Either that or the woman was as thick as a sack of *poha.*

"So tell me," she said, "all moved in? Are your rooms big enough? Is the air conditioner working well? Barstow is hot by day, cool by night. Be sure to shut it off."

We bobbed our heads up and down, raised our eyebrows. Rif even gave her the thumbs-up sign. We didn't tell our grandmother that her son had installed the refrigerator in the living room, right next to the couch, and announced, "Anyone moves this, I'll cut off his or her arm." We didn't tell her where he told the *Trailer Life* photographer to shove his camera, either.

As the spectacle of our first family dinner played out in front of me, I found myself stealing glances at the old lady with the bright red hair. She had the same nose as my dad's, same cowlick in the left front of her hairline. I imagined her holding my father in her arms when he was a baby, singing lullabies to him. Had she made his favorite meals for his birthday? Did she kiss his boo-boos when he fell off his bike? Did he bury his head in her chest and weep when his father died? Did my father grow up in a trailer park?

I also found myself searching Nana's face for similarities to my own face. Would I look like her when I was old?

Suddenly, I felt mad all over again. Having a weird grandmother was better than having no grandmother at all! I've been robbed! Isn't it some form of child abuse to tell your kids their nana is dead, then spring her on them fourteen years later?

Dad interrupted my thoughts with another loud burp.

"My goodness, Lance, where are your table manners?" his mother asked.

"My name is Lot," Dad said. "Don't call me Lance again."

Nana looked hurt. Mom looked annoyed. And everyone pretty much resumed chewing and not talking to one another after that.

The only bright side to my family's insanity was the fact that it was a great distraction. With my parents feuding, I didn't have time to dwell on my own dismal life. I didn't have time to miss Nadine or Fernando High or Mr. Puente's lame jokes about geometric theorems. I didn't have the energy to worry about turning into white trash or being hated by everybody at the new school I was starting in the morning whether I liked it or not.

"Save room for dessert," Nana said, finally. "I made tiramisù."

I stifled a groan. Why me? That's what I thought over and over. Why, of all the kids in the world, did everything awful happen to *me*?

chapter seventeen

The *tap, tap, tap* of Mom's Press-On nails against my bedroom door woke me early the next morning. It was just light out, already hot. Mom held a wrapped box in her hands. She sat on the edge of my bed.

"I know this is hard on you, honey," she said quietly. "It's hard on all of us."

At first I thought I was dreaming. I didn't say anything, just kept my head on the pillow waiting to see where this dream would go. When Mom reached up and brushed the hair out of my eyes, I marveled at how real it felt.

"I have a present for you," she said. And I smiled, expecting the package to unwrap itself and reveal its contents to me.

"Don't you want it?" Mom asked.

Oh, yes, I thought. What is it, Mommy?

"Libby?" Mom shook my shoulder. "Are you awake?"

Startled, I looked at my mother. "Mom?" I asked. "Is that really you?"

She laughed. "Yes, silly. Who did you think it was? Santa?" She handed me the box. "For the first day of the rest of your life," she said.

Sitting up in bed, I was now fully awake. Reality came crashing down on my head—I was living in Barstow, in a trailer, about to start my first day at the worst school ever. Even the thought of seeing the gorgeous guy with the incredible hazel eyes didn't lift my spirits. Carefully, I unwrapped the gift (we always saved wrapping paper in our house) and opened the box. My mother beamed.

"Breakfast is at Nana's in fifteen minutes," she said, getting up from my bed. "I can't wait to see you in your new outfit." Then she kissed me on the forehead and left me alone in my new metal room.

Rest of my life, here I come.

Nana insisted on waiting for the school bus with us, even though the stop was directly in front of the entrance to the trailer park.

"We're old enough to stand alone," Rif attempted. We both knew there was no budging her. Nana had proudly pulled major strings to get the bus to pick us up right at the front gate of the trailer park. Dirk's school was across the street, lucky for him. She didn't know how embarrassing it was.

"No grandchild of mine is going to walk a million blocks to the school bus. I pay taxes."

"Really, Nana. You don't have to—"

"Yes, I *do*."

So she did. We were the only kids picked up at that spot. Apparently the other kids who lived in Sunset Park drove to school or walked. But Nana would have none of that. She stood between my brother and me, one arm around each shoulder. I wore the tacky new pastel-green frilly outfit Mom bought me from Wal-Mart. And brand-new matching pastel-green canvas shoes. Yeah, I know. My heart sank when I lifted the ensemble out of the box. Hadn't she ever even *looked* at her daughter? What gave her the idea I'd *ever* wear such a hokey outfit? No way was I going to make my first impression in a new school in pastels!

Still, I couldn't erase her face from my mind. That eager, hopeful, apologetic, loving, desperate look she'd given me as she sat on my bed, gift in hand. Her face reminded me that her life was ruined, too. We were *all* stuck in Barstow. I couldn't stomach hurting my mom's feelings by showing up at the breakfast table in jeans and a rumpled black T-shirt pulled out of the bottom of my suitcase.

So I wore it.

I looked like the nerd of the century.

And I brought my real clothes with me in my backpack so I could change the moment I got to school.

"Finally!" Nana took her hands off our shoulders and clapped them together.

Just over the crest of the hill, the familiar orange-yellow color rose like a hideous sunrise. We watched the bus driver put on his blinkers and flashers, practically taking out a billboard announcing he was pulling over to pick up the losers who lived in Sunset

Park. Nana stood like a peacock, a huge turquoise medallion hanging around her neck. My heart raced. I felt dizzy. Nana sealed our fate by loudly asking the bus driver, "When was your last drug test?"

The whole school bus erupted in laughter. My face burned so red it felt like a sunburn. Rif didn't care. He high-fived everyone as he pimp walked down the aisle to the back of the bus. Me, I simply tried not to barf as I kept my head down and searched for the first empty seat out of the corner of my eye.

"Who's *that*?" I heard some guy ask.

"Nobody," another guy answered.

Recognizing the voice, I glanced up. It was *him*. The soulful blond boy who'd given Juan Dog back to me the day before. The boy I thought I might one day seriously kiss. When he caught me looking at him he said, "Keep moving. You're not sitting with me."

I wanted to cry. I wanted to explain how this had happened, how my life had veered wildly off course and careened into Barstow. I wanted to pull my clothes out of my pack and show everyone who I really was. I longed to turn the clock back to last year, when I was happy and didn't even know it. Instead, I watched my grandmother waving at me out the back window as she shrunk to a tiny turquoise dot in the bus's exhaust. Then I grabbed an empty seat in the back and stared at my fingernails.

"Nobody wants to sit with me, either." A girl's voice in front of me jolted me back to reality. I looked up. She said, "I'm Barbara Carver. It's okay. *I'll* be your friend."

Ah, geez.

Every high school has a Barbara Carver. She's a five-time

loser: overweight, acne, braces, glasses, and bad hair. No, make that *awful* hair. Barbara gathered a tuft of hair on top of her head into an old rubber band; it shot straight into the air like Old Faithful. Her fingernails were chewed so ferociously they were ten bloody half-moons.

I gulped. "Thanks. I'm Libby Madrigal." Then I settled into the bus seat and imagined how nice it would feel if the vinyl seat opened up and swallowed me whole.

Barbara stood, swung around, plopped down beside me and chatted all the way to school.

". . . so if you want to join a club, you pretty much have to organize it yourself."

"Uh-huh."

"And sports, like there's football and stuff. But if you want a really cool sport, like chess, you have to organize that yourself, too."

"Uh-huh."

As Barbara Carver filled me in on the limitations of Desert Valley High, I felt more and more woozy. My head was doing loop de loops. Each time I took in a breath, I felt dizzy when I exhaled. Hang on, girl, I repeated over and over in my head. Hang on. Everything's going to be okay.

We rode past Wal-Mart, through downtown, hung a right after the police station. My ears were hissing. By the time we passed the same tired old taco stand I'd passed several times the day before, I could barely hear Barbara at all. My ears were filled with the sound of the ocean. My upper lip was damp with sweat.

". . . so you want to stay away from them. I mean, like they are totally bad news."

Barbara continued her monologue, but all I heard was *whoosh!* All I felt was dizziness and a growing sense of panic.

The bus lurched to a stop, the door swung open. "Careful getting off, kids," the driver said. "No pushing."

Standing shakily, I let the crowd sweep me along in its current. My vision was blurred, I saw twinkling white lights. In the next horrible instant I felt like throwing up. Saliva flooded my mouth. The more I swallowed, the more liquid came rushing in. My stomach churned.

"Are you okay?" Barbara asked behind me. But her voice sounded so small and faraway I didn't think she was talking to me. My heart raced as my stomach lurched closer to upchucking the egg-white omelet Nana'd made for breakfast. I grabbed for my backpack. Lunch, and my non-nerdy clothes, were the only things inside it. I figured I could barf on Nana's smoked turkey wrap and suffer the additional humiliation of wearing my pastel ensemble all day. If I stuck my head far enough inside my pack, I could hurl and no one would even know. Dizzy, nauseous, and nearly off the deep end in terror, I fumbled with the clasp.

"Move your butt," someone yelled to me. It sounded like Rif.

"Shut up," Barbara snapped back.

"I wasn't talking to you, crater face."

"Good one, Shakespeare. Got any more original lines?"

Somehow I made it to the door. The bus steps were blurry. The crashing waves in my ears were now deafening. My hand clutched my stomach. Inch by inch, I managed to crawl down the bus steps. My knees didn't give way until I stepped onto the sidewalk. There, I folded like an accordion right into the gutter.

"Step over her!"

That's the last thing I heard before my head smacked the pavement.

"It looks worse than it is, Mrs. Madrigal," I heard the nurse tell my mom over the phone. That's when I reached up to feel my head. An enormous bandage covered the right half of my forehead, almost into my eye. It felt like a bath sponge.

"A nasty scrape," the nurse said to me, hanging up the phone. "You fainted. You'll be fine."

"Did I throw up?" I asked, wondering if I not only had to drop out of school in disgrace but move out of California, too.

"No. You just passed out."

I nearly fainted again when the nurse helped me into a sitting position, and I saw my reflection in the mirror across the room. "Can I have a Band-Aid instead of this . . . this . . . *maxi pad* on my forehead?"

"It's a *bandage*, and you'll need it if you start bleeding again," she said efficiently. "Do you have a headache?"

"No."

"Good. Any dizziness?"

"No."

"Nausea? Blurred vision?"

"No. I'm okay now." Even my heart had returned to its normal beat. "I think it was just a slight panic attack."

"Fine," the nurse said. "Then you can go to class."

That's not what I expected to hear. Suddenly I remembered, yeah, I did have a headache. "Can't I go home?" I asked. "Now that you mention it, my head does feel a little achy."

"Your mom said you should go to class if you could," said the nurse. "And I think you can."

My mom?! What did she know about my body? My mortification? The fact that my life was truly over if I started the first day of my new high school dressed like a lime-green mathlete with a *pillow* taped to my forehead!

"Here," said the nurse. "Let me help you to your feet."

Gripping my arm, the nurse supported me while I stood up. "If you bleed beyond the bandage or feel sick at all today, come back in," she said.

Before I could protest, the nurse patted my shoulder and released me into the wilds of Desert Valley High.

Mr. Tilden asked the class, "Who knows the difference between a metaphor and a simile?"

I knew his name because it was written on the class schedule I held in my trembling hand. I heard his question because I was standing, frozen, outside the closed door of my second period English class. The doorknob was inches away from my hand, but I couldn't bring myself to reach out and turn it. My heart pounded wildly. Trickles of sweat dribbled down into the cotton bandage on my forehead. As I took one tiny step forward, my too-new green canvas shoes squeaked on the exterior cement sidewalk. My backpack sagged against my rear end. Considering waiting it out, I looked at my watch. Then I looked at my schedule. There were still twenty minutes left before the end of class. No way could I wait it out just standing there. Or could I? Maybe now would be a good time to go to the bathroom and change my clothes?

"Door locked?"

My head jerked up. A custodian with a million keys hanging from his belt walked purposefully for the door.

"Well, I . . ."

Before I could say more, he tested the knob and the door opened easily. Annoyed, he said, "You've got to actually *turn* the knob, missy."

"I'm new," I stammered. Then I reached up to touch my bandage as some sort of explanation.

He softened, led me into the classroom. "Knobs turn to the *right*," he said slowly. The eruption of class laughter made me wish I could hide my whole body beneath that bandage. The custodian patted my shoulder just as the nurse had done and left.

"Can I help you, young lady?" Mr. Tilden asked.

"I'm in your class," I said. But my voice was so dinky I barely heard it.

"Pardon?"

Gulping, I took two steps further into the class. The moment I was in full view, no one said a word. It was the silence of curiosity, of alarm, of contempt. The walk to Mr. Tilden's desk felt longer than the trip to Barstow, and twice as hideous. If my legs were working properly, I would have turned around and run . . . all the way back to Chatsworth.

"Are you in my class?" Mr. Tilden asked.

I nodded. Handed him my note from the nurse. He read it, nodded himself, then looked at me with pity. To make matters worse, Mr. Tilden gently put his arm on my back and led me to a desk like I was an invalid. To make matters the worst they could possibly be, he said, "Brian, could you please get up and give Elizabeth your desk?"

"It's Libby," I squeaked. But I'm sure no one heard because Brian, some grubby-looking guy in the front row, groaned and said, "I thought gimps go in the back."

chapter eighteen

Nana walked Rif to the front gate of Sunset Park the next morning. I stayed home. I blinked a lot and told Mom I had a horrific
headache, blurred vision, and dizziness. None of it was true, of
course. But, man, I deserved a day off. Maybe the whole semester. Enduring the first day at my new high school dressed like a
suburban mom with a giant white turban on her forehead was
more than any fourteen-year-old should be required to bear.

My first day had been one humiliation after another. Barbara
Carver was the only person who said a word to me all day. And,
like some demented sports announcer, she ran the instant replay
reel over and over.

". . . and there you were, splat, in the gutter! You passed out!
Splat!"

I felt like a virus spreading through campus. As I moved
toward groups of giggling kids, they clammed up, looked away,
melted off. No one wanted to get near me. Like they might

catch me or something.

". . . and there was blood on the sidewalk and everything!" squealed Barbara. *"Spalat!"*

"I'll make chicken soup," Nana declared, once she heard I was staying home from school.

"Hmm?" Mom wasn't paying attention because she had a job interview at Wal-Mart, and Dad, bizarrely, decided to spend his day on the couch watching soap operas in Spanish.

"Ella tiene un problema con su espina."

"¡No!"

"Sí. No tiene sensibilidad en sus piernas."

"¡No!"

"Sí."

Just when you think your family can't get any weirder.

So Nana scuttled off to her kitchen, Mom waddled to the bathroom to shellac her hair with hair spray, and Dad reached his arm up from the couch to open the refrigerator and pull out a six-pack of cola.

"I'm feeling a little less dizzy," I said, though no one even came close to caring.

Since I knew Nana's chicken soup would begin with an actual *chicken*, I figured I had at least half an hour before anyone noticed whether I was dead or alive. I decided to take a walk, work off a few extra calories so I could eat a noodle or two. All the kids would be at school; I wouldn't "infect" anyone.

Reading my mind, Juan Dog stared hopefully in my direction, licking his tiny lips.

"Okay, you can come."

Thrilled, Juan Dog leaped off Dad's lap and ran to my feet.

"I'm taking Juan for a walk, Dad."

"Bueno." His eyes never left the tube.

Stifling hot air swallowed me up the moment I stepped into the glaring Barstow sun. I lowered Juan Dog to the pavement and watched him sniff and hop around, his tiny feet scorched on the scalding cement.

"You asked for it," I said.

My forehead was already sweating into my bandage. My lungs even felt hot. But soon, as before, the dry heat felt good. It calmed me, in spite of myself.

"Get your *head* wet, Gracie!"

A female voice floated on the air as Juan and I passed Eden Way on the way to the pool.

"The water isn't going to bite you, Gracie!"

The same two old women I'd seen the last time were there. Charlotte was wearing her signature straw hat; Mim's skin still rippled like cake batter. They were both standing at the edge of the pool shouting to another old woman who doggy-paddled her way through the deep end, the rubber flowers on her bathing cap flapping with each pawing stroke. "Stick your head in and swim, for heaven's sake!"

Gracie continued bobbing; Charlotte and Mim kept yelling at her. "Your head! Dunk it!" As I quietly circled around the fence to the other end of the pool area, I saw an old man in a wheelchair parked near the shallow-end steps, clapping his hands together and grinning. His smile was all gums.

Yip!

"Shhh, Juan!"

Yip, yip! Excited by the action, Juan Dog barked again. *Yip!*

Charlotte jerked her head up and shrieked, "It's the grand-child and the puppy!" She trudged over, swung open the gate, and flagged me in.

"Got your suit on?" she asked.

"No, I was just taking a walk," I said.

"Nonsense! Get in here."

"What's that on your forehead?" Gracie shouted from the side of the pool.

I shouted back, "A bandage. I fell."

"Concussion?" she asked.

"No," I said. Gracie shrugged and resumed doggy-paddling.

Mim called from the far end of the pool. "Did you *bring* your swimsuit?"

"Um, no."

"That's okay. I have an extra in my locker." She turned and lumbered into the rec room.

"No . . . thanks . . . really . . ."

Charlotte said, "I'll mind the little one while you swim." Then she snatched Juan right out of my arms. Startled, I warned again, "He doesn't like strangers." But just as he'd done with Mim before, Juan nestled his little head into the drape of flesh beneath Charlotte's chin and went right to sleep.

"Well, he sure likes me," she sniffed. I felt betrayed. The little runt.

"Here it is!" Mim sang, returning poolside dangling a turquoise-and-orange flowered one-piece that was obviously sev-eral sizes too big for me, not to mention too hideous to wear.

"I don't really swim," I said lamely.

"Nonsense!" said Charlotte.

"There's nothing to it," Gracie called from the pool. To prove it, she pushed off from the edge and took a full ten minutes to reach the other side. The old man in the wheelchair clapped and made weird smacking noises with his gums.

"It oughta fit you just fine." Mim held the bathing suit up and squinted. Apparently she was blind, or in major denial about her size. "You're welcome to borrow it."

"And the pool's just been cleaned," Charlotte added, stroking Juan's head and murmuring, "there, there." Juan was softly snoring like a little sewing machine. *Rat, tat, tat.*

"Thanks, but I was just exploring."

"Why not explore the deep end?" Gracie shoved off again and doggy-paddled across. The old man clapped again.

"As soon as school lets out, I was hoping to find some kids my age."

Charlotte, Mim, and Gracie glanced at each other then exploded in laughter. "Kids her age!" The man in the wheelchair erupted in a silent, toothless laugh.

"Or college age," I mumbled, trying to sound mature. That made them laugh even harder.

"Hon, this is a retirement home," said Charlotte.

Despite the heat, my insides froze. Strangely, the lapping of the water became louder than Charlotte's voice. Still, I heard her repeat, "A *retirement* home." It echoed in deep slow motion: *Re . . . ti . . . re . . . ment . . . hooommme.*

Gracie offered helpfully, "Irene what's-her-name on Paradise Way is only sixty-two."

"A retirement home?"

"Didn't your grandmother tell you?"

"A retir—"

"The only reason they let you live here is because your grandma built this rec center."

Suddenly, it was hard to breathe.

"She invested almost all of your grandpa's life insurance money right here in Sunset Park!"

"Last year, we added a DVD theater!" Gracie yelled from the pool.

Charlotte said, "Your grandmother helped make Sunset Park one of the most desirable mobile retirement homes in the area. There's a waiting list a mile long."

"Some of us simply refuse to expire." Gracie giggled.

"They squeezed your family in at the head of the line."

Stunned, I tried to move but couldn't.

Charlotte said, "Why not take a dip, hon? Like I said, the pool's just been cleaned."

"This suit oughta fit you just fine," Mim repeated, shoving in into my hands.

In a surge of desperate energy, I crammed the bathing suit under my arm, yanked Juan Dog from Charlotte's chins, and bolted for the gate.

Gracie yelled after me. "Look! I can dunk my head!"

The gate slammed shut behind me. The last thing I heard was Charlotte shouting, "No running around the pool!"

chapter eleven

I staged a hunger strike. It was the only way I could protest force-fully enough. Slowly, I'd waste away. Nourishment would pass these lips only when my parents restored the life they stole from me. I'd stop the secrets and lies right here, right now.

On the outside of my slammed bedroom door, I posted a sign that read NO FOOD. NO WATER. NO VISITORS. To my astonishment, everyone obeyed. I lay there for hours. It was the first time my family ever did what I asked them to do. Nana didn't even attempt to deliver her promised chicken soup.

Just before noon, Mom poked her head in. About time, I thought.

"Guess what?" she said.

"What?" I asked indignantly.

"I got the job! I start tomorrow! The jewelry counter. Can you believe it? It's the best department in Wal-Mart. They have a new shipment of cubic zirconia coming in. Guess who is in charge of arranging the display case."

"Congratulations," I said, my voice dripping with sarcasm.

"Thanks, sweetie. You sure you don't want anything to eat or drink?"

Defiantly I stated, "Yes. I'm absolutely sure. No way am I eating a single solitary bite or drinking a sip."

"Okay, then. I'm off to get a manicure. I want my nails to look *perfect* when I show customers our new line."

Mom left and I fell back on my bed. What was *wrong* with these people? What good is a hunger strike if no one notices?

Feeling utterly powerless, I did the only thing I could do under the circumstances: I waited until I heard the screen door close behind my mother's rear end, and I snuck in the living room to find the cell phone Dad had hidden. Our regular phone wasn't installed yet, and, in retaliation for his forced sobriety, Dad had forbidden us from using his cell.

"We're a family," he'd said. "We'll suffer together."

Finding his phone was a piece of cake. Spanish soap operas blared on the television. Dad was asleep and snoring on the couch, an empty cola can rising and falling atop his rounded gut. I tiptoed into my parents' bedroom and searched through Dad's dresser. Bingo. I found his phone in five minutes flat.

"Nadine?" The moment I knew school was out and her cell was on, I dialed my best friend's number.

"Libby!" she screamed. "How are you?"

"Life sucks," I said, borrowing a phrase from my brother.

As I was taking a breath to fill Nadine in on all the hideous details of my hideous new life, she said, "I miss you so much! I've been dying to talk to you! Thank God you have a phone. What's your new number?"

Before I could take a breath, she was off and babbling again. "Curtis and his older brother and I went to Zuma Beach Monday after school and it was so cool. The sun was hot and Curtis looked even hotter in his wetsuit. I so wish you were there. He surfs! Did you know that?"

"No, uh—"

"School is a nightmare without you. My whole day is dismal. How's your new school? Fernando High is exactly the same old drag."

"You think *Fernando* is a drag," I began.

"Just a minute!" I heard Nadine shout to someone, then to me she said, "I can't believe this! I have to go. My ride is here. Paige's mom is dropping us off at the mall."

"Paige?" My heart fell to the floor.

"You remember Paige Dalton? She's great. You'd like her."

Paige Dalton was a cheerleader. Paige was friends with Carrie Taylor. How had my best friend become friends with Paige Dalton in less than a week?

"Paige is friends with Curtis. That's how we met."

Ah.

"Can I call you later?" Nadine asked, obviously impatient to get off the phone. "What's your new number?"

"We don't have a phone yet. I'll call you."

"Oh, Libby. I miss you *so* much."

"I miss you too, Na—"

"I'm coming!" Nadine hollered to the gaggle of girls I could hear in the background.

"I have to go, too," I said loudly. "My friend Barbara Carver is showing me around Barstow tonight."

There. That'll get her.

"Awesome," Nadine said sincerely. "When we get our driver's licenses, we can all hang out."

I tried not to feel the sting. I could hear Nadine climbing into Paige Dalton's mother's car. Digging my fingernails into the hard plastic of the phone, I said, "Our new house is amazing. There are lots of cool kids around here, too. They hang out at this old landmark McDonald's in a bunch of railroad cars. You *have* to see it. It's awesome. And my school, well, there's so much going on I don't know when I'll have the time to do homework."

"Wow, Libby. I thought you said your life sucks."

"Yeah, well, that was just an expression. Kids say that . . . around here . . . when they think something is, um, good." I winced.

"Ah." I didn't fool Nadine for a second. Which made me feel even more humiliated. I wanted to delete the past five minutes, start over.

"Call me?" Nadine asked sweetly.

I swallowed. "Sure."

"Luv ya."

"I love you, too," I said, trying not to sound as desperate as I felt. The silence pierced straight through to my heart. Nadine was gone, off with her cheerleading, mall-shopping friends. Soon to experience a serious kiss. Aware that her former best friend was a liar. Falling back on my bed, tears flowed like the tide at Zuma Beach.

The next morning, I refused to get out of bed. I lay there beneath my covers, the air conditioner blowing full blast, Juan Dog curled up at my feet like a hairy, big-eared snail.

Mom knocked. "You okay, Libbydoodle?"

"Yeah, *right.*"

"How's your head?"

"My *head* is fine," I growled.

"Good. I'm off to work!"

I said nothing. No way was I going to reply, "Have a good day!" Not when my parents had moved me into a *retirement* home, for heaven's sake. Not when my own mother didn't notice that I was starving to death and refusing to go to school. What kind of parents did I have? I could lapse into coma! What did they care? As I lay beneath the covers, my stomach rumbling, I considered never talking to anybody again. What was the point? My life was over.

"Wish me luck!" Mom sang. Then she vanished without waiting for me to wish her anything. Not that I would wish her anything good. Not in a million years.

Shortly after I heard the front door slam three times, I heard the refrigerator door open and a *pfftt* sound as Dad plopped down on the couch and popped open a soda can. Then I heard voices.

"So you claim he promised to pay for the damage?"

"I never promised to pay!"

Apparently, Dad had shifted from watching Spanish soaps to watching Judge Judy.

"I have him on tape!"

Feeling majorly depressed, I sank into the mattress, determined never to get up again. To pass the time, I slathered lotion on my arms and smeared some on Juan's head, making his little hairs stick straight up in spikes.

"Anybody home?" Someone was on the other side of the door, tapping softly.

"Go away," I grumbled.

"Okay." It was Nana. I heard her footsteps walking away.

"What do you want?" I called, loud. The footsteps returned.

"I brought you a little something."

"What is it?"

"Can I come in?"

I sighed. "All right."

Nana opened the door, entered, and shut the door behind her. She held a plate in her hand, covered by one of those metal warmers they use for room service in fancy hotels. "Thought you might be hungry," she said. Did I smell butter and garlic? Something green . . . basil, maybe?

"I'm not," I lied. The aroma of whatever lay beneath the metal cover was unbelievably alluring. My mouth drowned my tongue in saliva.

"My mistake." Nana quietly turned to leave with my food in her hands. Man, she was good.

"My life is *over*," I declared.

Nana turned back and sat next to me on the bed. "How much longer do you have?"

Groaning, I asked, "Why won't anyone take me seriously?"

"I'm sorry, Libby. Do you want to talk about it?"

"No."

"I'm sorry about that, too." She made another motion to leave. What was *wrong* with this family? Didn't anyone care that I was wasting away to dust?

"If you change your mind, I'll be in my kitchen making grilled scallops over frisée for lunch," Nana said, placing the plate on my desk and reaching for the doorknob.

"How *could* they?!" I blurted out.

"How could who?"

"How could my parents move us into a retirement home?!"

"Ah." Nana returned and settled herself on the edge of my bed. "I was wondering when you'd notice all the wrinkles around here."

"How *could* they?"

"Do your brothers know?"

"I don't think so." Though Rif had noticed that the speed limit inside the trailer park was fifteen miles per hour, and most drivers drove ten.

"What were they thinking? I mean, my parents might as well have moved us into a convent!"

"Is it that bad?"

"It's just so . . . so . . ." I stopped. How could I tell my grandmother how I really felt? This was her home, after all. How could I tell her I didn't want to live with a bunch of old farts? In a trailer? The humiliation of it! Would Nana ever understand how much my family embarrassed me, how I begged God, "Please, don't let me become my mother?" Or how my own father—her son—made me feel so confused and unsafe? It's awful to watch my dad disappear into alcohol, to have to tiptoe around him, making sure no one says out loud what we're all thinking. My family hides, so no one will see him. We feel ashamed of ourselves because we're so ashamed of him.

How do you tell your newfound grandmother you feel

damaged? There are no words to express how much it hurts to see my dad all melted and drooling and baggy eyed. Why would a father let his daughter see him lose his manhood every day, fade into the couch and stop caring about his kids, and treat their mother like she's an intruder in his own private blurry world? Doesn't he realize I'll carry that image with me all my life? How am I ever supposed to have a boyfriend, or a fiancé, or a husband if my image of men is so warped?

The most unsettling thing of all, of course, is that my dad stopped drinking since we moved to Barstow (as far as I could tell), and he's as weird as ever.

My mouth hung open, but nothing came out. How could I tell an old woman what it's like to have your parents one day just decide to destroy your life? Without even asking. To *ruin* your whole entire life without even saying sorry! My best friend has already traded me in for a better model. All the boys I've ever liked like somebody else. Greg Minsky freaks me out, and Zack Nash looks at me like I'm his little sister. Like I'm invisible! And now I'll never get the one thing I really want: a serious kiss. It's too late. I'm branded a loser for *life*.

How could I express how terrified I was to start over in a new school? My whole life is one giant hold button — *blinking, blinking, blinking*–waiting for whatever dreadful thing is going to happen next.

Nana reached her veiny, ring-encrusted hand up to tuck a strand of hair behind my ear. She sighed. "Sometimes there's so much to say it's hard to find even one word."

I nodded.

She said, "It's a funny thing, though. Teens and old people

171

have a lot in common."

Staring at her, I struggled not to roll my eyes and grunt.

"Old age scares people," she said softly, "so they don't like to see it. They herd all of us into retirement homes, pretend not to hear us when we talk. Younger people treat older people like children. We feel powerless much of the time, our bodies are giving out, doing bizarre things they never did before. Betraying us. But you can only share what's happening with other old people—who else wants to hear about constipation and arthritis and bunions? Certainly, no one wants to hear about bladder control. It's a joke on Jay Leno! That's how society feels about us—people are so scared of becoming us, they can only mention us in jest. Really, society barely tolerates old folks. Sound familiar?"

I nodded, blinked. Of all people, I thought my grandmother would be the *last* to understand.

"It's lonely being old," Nana continued. "You're invisible. Men are not attracted to you; women cling too tightly. And there's that cloud that follows you around night and day: Will this year be my last? Have I done enough with my life? Will I be missed?"

Nana stared off into space for a moment. Suddenly, in her face, I could see the woman she once was. The fiery widow who declared, "To hell with what others think of me, I'm living in a kitchen!"

"It's true," I said quietly, "society barely tolerates both of us."

Smiling, Nana took my hand and squeezed it. "I tell you one thing, my love," she said. "It's a secret that's taken me seventy-five years to discover."

"What?" Straining, I lifted my head off the pillow.

"*No one* has any control."

"Nobody?" I let my head fall back down.

"Nope. Control is only an illusion. Striving for it is a waste of time. Life itself has a plan for you that's playing out right now, on its own, without your intervention. No matter what you do, life is going to win. You cannot control it. It's foolish to try. You've got to *let go*. Let life's flow carry you along in its current. Don't resist. Sit back and enjoy the ride. Watch where life takes you. Stop trying to steer it. Life will always win, my darling. Give it up. Let go."

Nana stroked my cheek, then leaned over to kiss me on the only patch of my forehead that wasn't covered by a now-filthy white gauze. In my ear she whispered, "In the meantime, you might want a little snack."

My grandmother left me with a wicked frittata and a big surprise: I wasn't so alone after all.

chapter twenty

I awoke the next morning with a new resolve. To let go.

"Whatcha making?" Mom asked me as I stood at Nana's stove, dots of flour on my old T-shirt, my forehead bandage left atop my unmade bed.

"Pancakes."

"Pancakes?"

"Want a stack?"

Mom looked alarmed, not sure what to say.

I slid the spatula beneath the bubbling batter and flipped one of the cakes. Mom sat at the table and asked, "Are you okay?"

"Never better. Butter?"

The enormous pancake stack slanted and wiggled as I carried it to the table. Nana and my brothers had already eaten; in fact, they were already gone. Off somewhere living their lives, going to school. Me, I was letting life carry me in its current.

"Syrup, Mom?"

"You seem well enough to go to school, Libby," she said.

"We'll see."

Life wanted me to stay home for the rest of the week.

"Libby—"

"You're going to be late for work, Mom."

My mother glanced up at the clock, said, "Oh, dear," and rushed back to our trailer. I settled in for the most delicious pancake breakfast I'd ever eaten. Juan whined beneath the table, but I pushed him aside with my foot. Cutting little pancake triangles with my fork, I shoved several layers into my mouth at a time. Letting go never tasted so good.

After breakfast, I decided to forgo a shower. I let go of bathing, too. Why bother? Who cared if I was dirty or clean? My head was fine. A brown scab covered pink, tender skin. It didn't hurt, just itched a little. Sliding my bare feet into thongs, I wore the same boxer shorts I'd slept in, scooped up Juan Dog, and left.

It didn't take long to make my way to the pool. As I approached, I could hear the same chatter and lazy slapping of the water. Charlotte wasn't there yet, but Mim and the clapper in the wheelchair were, plus a new old lady who was totally bald. She swam slow, deliberate strokes back and forth across the pool. In my new frame of mind, they all looked stunning.

"Beautiful day!" I called out breezily as I walked through the gate.

"Good morning," Mim said, then she asked gently, "How are you, dear?"

"Never better. Happy as a clam. Snug as a bug in a rug. And you? How are your bunions?"

Mim looked startled. With Juan Dog in tow, I dropped myself

175

into an empty lounge and closed my eyes. The sun was already blistering hot and it was just past nine.

"Sunscreen, dear?" Mim asked. "The desert sun is treacherous." Eyes still closed, I shook my head no, stretched out. Listening to the gentle ripples in the pool, I imagined I was floating down a river on my back, destination unknown—letting go, letting life sweep me along in its current. What did I have to worry about anymore?

When we were little, Mom used to call Rif, Dirk, and me her three dwarfs: Breezy, Dopey, and Warty (me), as in worrywart. Then, who could blame me? I mean, who wouldn't worry, when life was always one big question mark? The way I figured it, I was the only one in my family who recognized how bad things can be, how many perils there are to life. The way I saw it, I was the only one who worried *appropriately.* But not anymore. From now on, Mom would call me her dwarf Bright Side. Or Floaty. Yeah, from now on I'd be Floaty, the girl who goes with the flow.

My sunburn was just surfacing when I returned to Nana's for lunch.

"Yikes," she said, taking one look at me. Then she reached past the sink to snap off a frond of aloe from her window box herb garden. Dirk, home for lunch, kept poking my arm to see his white fingerprint. Dad didn't even see me; he was staring at something imaginary crawling up the wall. "Will ya look at that," he said over and over. When Mom came in she winced and asked, "Want some *Noxemawema* for that?"

Shrugging everybody off, I sat down to eat. "What smells so good?"

"Grilled chicken and avocado wrap with pecorino romano

and garlic mayonnaise," Nana said, quietly rubbing aloe juice on my hot red arms and angry red forehead.

My eyes teared up with joy.

By evening, my eyelids were practically swollen shut. My lips were huge chorizo sausages and my thighs were blistered. Mom came into my bedroom and placed a cool, wet cloth over my face. She kissed my head.

"Poor little red riding face," she said.

I tried to smile beneath the face cloth, but my skin felt prickly and stiff. Soon I noticed it didn't hurt as much when I didn't move, when I lay flat on top of my bed in the blast of the air conditioner. Which is exactly what I did. All night. And the weekend, too. The only time I got up was to go to the bathroom.

Oddly, it felt as if I was watching myself instead of being myself. I didn't feel the sunburn as much as notice it. Briefly, I wondered why life had decided to singe my skin—particularly my lips, when I really needed them to taste Nana's food—but then I chalked it up to the Master Plan. How can you question a Master Plan? Besides, my old life was over anyway. Clearly, the new one included pain.

Mom appeared periodically with fresh face cloths, Nana with fresh food (cold, of course). Grateful, I tried to say "thank you" but my huge lips could only say "Fwank eh," so I chose to be silent. Until mealtimes, when Nana checked on me and I managed to lift my head and whisper, "Is there any honey-baked ham weft?"

My world shrunk to the size of my bedroom ceiling. I stared at it so long, it began to look like the white sands of Zuma Beach where Nadine romped in the waves without me.

chapter twenty-one

My face looked much less scary Monday morning.

"You going to school?" Mom asked.

"I doubt it." At Nana's breakfast table, I was devouring Cajun sausages and poached eggs.

"Let me rephrase that," Mom said. "You're going to school."

I looked up from my plate. "How can I let life flow in the confines of high school?"

Mom's face knotted itself into a mixture of exasperation and bewilderment. She said, "All I know is, you're going to flow your duff right onto that bus today. And you have twenty minutes to get ready."

Life told me I ought to listen to my mother or else.

Desert Valley High looked completely different to me. It was still ugly, but I didn't care. The low concrete buildings resembled bunkers huddled in the desert. Beyond the rusty chain-link fence, the Mojave spread out flat and wide over a mile to the foot of the dirt-brown mountains.

As I walked through campus in my green Wal-Mart shoes (what did I care?), I noticed that the biggest difference between Fernando and Desert Valley was the *atmosphere*. D.V. High was much more retro than my old school. The cafeteria (yes, there was one, but it was old and disgusting) served meat loaf sandwiches instead of Big Macs. Many of the male teachers had scruffy beards and wrinkled ties. Most of the women wore Birkenstocks. Teacher-wise, it's that kind of place: A school that time forgot. Student-wise, it was more like *Boyz N the Hood*, that old movie about South Central L.A. Lots of macho strutting and angling for position, the girls both scoffing at and standing by their *boyz*. I'm not saying it felt like there might be a drive-by or something. There weren't metal detectors or roving video cams. But there was a lot of posturing—guys and girls who stood around and sneered at everybody and thought they were more than cool. To me, with my new perspective, Desert Valley High School seemed like a decrepit old pit bull—more bark than bite, hopelessly past its prime but unwilling to admit it. I mean, nobody even rode skateboards. It's like they don't know what's going on in the outside world.

"Welcome back." Barbara Carver met me at my locker. It was so dented it looked like my old locker at Fernando.

"Thanks." I smiled at her, stashed the roasted red pepper and mozzarella sandwich Nana had made me, and headed for class.

"Meet me here at lunch, okay?"

"Okay," I said. What did I care? Barbara was as good a friend as any. At least she wouldn't dump me for a cheerleader in less than a week.

My pastel canvas shoes squeaked on the cement as I walked away. Across the quad, a guy with eyes as black as his hair was staring at me. I smiled, but he just nodded. His gaze made me feel like a walking X ray, as if he could see my rib cage expand with each breath. There was something about his intensity that made my face flush instantly. There was also something about him that made me feel good. His eyes weren't judging me, they were simply taking me in. Later that day, I found myself scanning the desks in all my classes, disappointed that he wasn't there.

Academically, I quickly discovered I could graduate from D.V. High in my sleep. Geometry? Forget about it. Who needed to know what a trapezoid was if Zack Nash wasn't the reward? I chose, instead, to take courses I knew I could ace and wear my "loser" label with straight-A pride.

Rif embraced our new high school like they were old war buddies or something. With Rif, it was easy. He simply fell into the group of bad boys. Rebels know how to spot one another instantly. Everywhere he went, guys in baggy army surplus clothes opened their ranks to include him. Everywhere I went, girls in tight tank tops tightened their circles to keep me out.

Except, of course, one girl.

"Follow me," Barbara Carver said at lunch.

"Where?" Not that I really cared. I just wanted to make sure I had enough time to eat. Nana had baked white chocolate brownies.

"Out," Barbara said.

Shrugging, I grabbed my lunch, slammed my locker, and plodded along beside her in the direction of the fence.

As we walked off campus, one student puffed his cheeks with air while his friend shouted, "Make room! It's an elephant and her roasted peanut!" Another yelled, "Nerds of a feather stick together."

That started a chain reaction.

"The Loser's Club!"

"Tubby and Cher!"

"*Lez* be friends!"

I was mortified. I'd never been taunted like that before. My resolve to let life flow dissolved into a desire to shove Barbara away and explain to the gathering crowd, "I'm not who you think I am. I'm in a slump, that's all. Haven't you ever had your life ripped out from under you? Haven't you ever felt like nobody understood you? Haven't you ever wanted to belong, but nobody would let you in?"

That's what I wanted to yell, so they would take a second look, stop judging me as the lame-o who fainted on her first day of school, wore a couch cushion on her head, and Wal-Mart canvas slip-ons on her feet because her family couldn't afford real sneakers. I longed to clarify the fact that *Barbara* befriended *me.* I was just going with the flow, you know?

"You talkin' to me?" Barbara yelled at one of the guys who made fun of us.

"Yeah, I'm talkin' to you, lard ass," the skinny boy yelled back.

"Ignore him, Barbara," I said, blushing for her. She ignored me instead.

"You talkin' to *me*?" she said again to the boy.

"If the ass fits, wear it," he said, doubling over with laughter.

Barbara dropped her backpack and hulked across the dead grass. The boy looked stricken but stood his ground. His friends were all around him. No way was he gonna run from a fat girl.

"Do you have any idea how lardy my ass really is?" Barbara asked him. "Do you have any notion how heavy I really am?"

I swallowed. Or tried to.

Stunned, the boy said, "Like, it's so obvious. You're, like, *huge*."

"Huge, huge," she repeated, her fingers rubbing her chin. "So hard to define exactly what the word 'huge' really means." Then her face lit up. "I know! I'm going to show you. I'm going to let you feel how huge I really am. So you'll know, you'll know forever."

In one surprisingly agile wrestling move, she sat on him. Barbara pinned the guy on the dry grass in the middle of the quad. Red faced, he wriggled beneath her girth. It was the most hilarious thing I'd ever seen. His friends were hysterical with laughter. A bigger crowd gathered. I glanced around for the boy I'd seen earlier, but he wasn't there. Barbara sang at the top of her voice, "Can you feel it?" as she pressed her lard ass on top of him.

"Get off me!"

"Say *please*."

"Move your butt, you tub of lard!"

"I didn't hear the magic word." Barbara didn't budge. The skinny kid looked like he might suffocate. The rest of the kids were actually cheering for Barbara now.

"Flatten him, lard ass!" one of the Sylvanas squealed.

"Get *off*!!" The boy screeched. Then, in a breathless, butt-

182

squished voice he added, "Please!"

Barbara got up, dusted her hands off, and said, "I just had a baby-sitting job!"

Everybody roared, Barbara bowed. And I felt a feeling I hadn't even come close to feeling since we arrived in Barstow: pride. As unexpected as snow atop a cactus, I felt proud that Barbara Carver was my friend.

"The best part of Barstow is on the wrong side of the tracks."

Barbara took me on a tour. "Hurry up," she said. "We only have an hour."

Practically running, I followed Barbara Carver down a side street gritty with sand. The midday sun was blistering. I'd decided to help life give me a break and slathered sunscreen all over my face while we hurried across Main Street.

"This side is where all the hideous fast-food places are, the tourist motels, the Wal-Mart."

"My mother works at Wal-Mart," I said, ashamed.

"Everyone's mother works at Wal-Mart!"

I beamed. "Yours, too?"

Barbara kept walking fast. "No. My *step*mother works at Wal-Mart. My real mother lives in New York with her boyfriend."

"Oh." I didn't know what else to say, which was okay when I was with Barbara Carver, because she always did.

"I'm hoping to follow in my mother's footsteps and find a boyfriend who moves me to New York, too. I'd even accept Victorville or Palmdale. Just as long as it's not here. And as long as he's a real boyfriend, not one of those serial killers who pretends to be in love with you so you'll get in his car. I mean, how low can you sink? Your first ever boyfriend is a serial killer?"

I just looked at her. What do you say to that?

"The wrong side of the tracks is the real Barstow." Barbara blathered on. "If you hurry, we can have lunch at my favorite spot."

"I brought lunch," I said.

"Not like this," she replied.

We continued downhill until we passed an old, long brick building.

"That's the Mother Road Museum," Barbara said. "Boring, unless you like railroad stuff and Route Sixty-six memorabilia."

"What's the big whoop about Route Sixty-six anyway?" I asked.

"It's like one long road almost all the way across the country. They call it 'the Main Street of America.' I guess it was pretty cool when they didn't have freeways. Now, it's just a way to get tourists to drive through small, crappy towns."

I nodded and wiped the sweat off my forehead with the back of my hand.

"That's what I call Big Moe," Barbara said, pointing to a huge, lumpy rock in the dry Mojave River bed across from the museum. "Little Moe is over there."

"You name rocks?"

"What else is there to do around here?"

I laughed.

Barbara chugged over an old iron bridge across a nonexistent river. I couldn't help but think she was incredibly fast for a chubette. I struggled to keep up. Along the way, she announced points of interest.

"Rainbow Basin, down there, is where lots of fossils are.

"Calico Ghost Town is an old miner's town. Kind of hokey but interesting for newbies.

"Ancient Aborigines once lived in that valley."

Amazingly, Barbara Carver made Barstow sound sort of interesting.

When we finally got over the bridge, past the railroad tracks, Barstow changed completely. It felt like we were in a giant sandbox dotted with dried-up weeds. Where the other side of Barstow had seemed dead, this side seemed dead and buried. The houses looked more like sheds. There wasn't a flame-broiled burger in sight. Instead, Barbara led me into a tiny shack with a hand-painted sign that read AQUÍ.

"We're here," Barbara said. "Literally."

I knew enough Spanish to get the joke. Barbara knew enough to order, *"Lo mismo. Para dos."* She explained that she eats there several times a week, always the same, always *lo mismo.*

"What did you order?" I asked.

"You'll see," she said.

The smell of cilantro and onions made my mouth water. I forgot all about Nana's sandwich, let life flow me to the only table inside. Outside, dusty construction workers sat at picnic tables in the sun or in their trucks, eating burritos and drinking *cervezas.*

"I'm buying today," Barbara said. "Next time lunch is on you."

I didn't argue. Especially after I bit into the burrito she handed me. My mouth exploded with flavor. It was smoky and spicy, with grilled steak, melted cheese, fresh salsa, avocado, and lime. It tasted so good, I wanted to bury my face in the warm flour tortilla.

"Welcome to my Barstow," Barbara said, grinning while she chewed.

chapter twenty-two

My family settled in pretty quickly. Which got me thinking about life in general. You sleep, eat, do homework, go to school, hang out, watch TV, go to bed. The details are the only difference. Which, of course, make all the difference in the world.

That night, I slipped into feeling sorry for myself again. I missed Nadine, Zack Nash, and even Greg Minsky. Barbara made me laugh, but she wasn't my *best* friend. Best friends know all your secrets and love you anyway. I still felt too embarrassed to even invite Barbara over. I still had tons of secrets to keep.

The big secret, of course—the whopper that no one in my family dared reveal—was the fact that my dad wasn't much different now that he was sober. He guzzled colas instead of beers. He sat slumped in his chair all day, eyes bleary from watching nonstop TV. He grumbled at my mother, ignored us, told Juan Dog to shut up, burped. The father I once knew—funny, loving, *there*—was still gone. It began to look like he was gone for good.

That night, I lay flat on my bed, facedown, and—even though I tried not to—cried myself to sleep.

Each week, I spent part of my allowance at Aquí. Unbelievably, I didn't get fat. The explosion of blubber I feared, once I let myself actually eat, never materialized. My stomach stopped growling—that was the biggest change in my body. Pretty soon, it dawned on me that food wasn't the enemy after all. *Over*eating was. I could actually have breakfast, lunch, and dinner and not turn into my mom! Unless, of course, I ate like a lumberjack or a fast-food fiend, and I was neither. Feeling healthy actually felt good.

Getting to know Barbara Carver felt good, too.

"Popularity in high school doesn't mean squat," she said one day on our way to Aquí. "Just ask Johnny Depp. They used to call him Johnny *Dip*."

Barbara didn't care what anyone thought of her. She told me, "It's a choice you have to make. Are you going to give some dumb teenagers power over your self-esteem? Or are you going to empower yourself and become whomever you want to become?"

When she wasn't cracking me up, she was saying deep stuff like that. And using cool words like "empower" and "whomever." I'd never met anyone who had so many things to feel insecure about but felt totally secure anyway. Just hanging out with her made me start to see things differently. Like, my happiness just might be in my very own hands. Even when bad things happened, I didn't have to be depressed *forever*.

Incredibly, life's Master Plan was flowing me into a less

stressed-out space. Though Nadine was a hundred and forty miles away, my serious kiss was light-years away, and my former self was a quickly fading memory, I had Barbara and burritos and air-conditioning and Nana's cooking and Juan Dog's huge, silky ears.

chapter twenty-three

You'd think I would have been thrilled to get out of school for the day; you'd think I would have been honored to make Desert Valley High's Most Promising Students list so quickly. But the truth was, my new high school was filled with so many dunces, I could get straight A's with my brain tied behind my back. And the field trip they gave the thirty of us on the list seemed like home-work to me. A geology walk? Through a humongous rock forma-tion called Devil's Punchbowl? Right next to the San Andreas Fault? Why couldn't they reward our brainpower with a bus trip in the other direction—to Las Vegas?

"Wear hiking shoes and layered clothing," Mr. Rhinehart, the Earth Sciences teacher and leader of our expedition, said. "It's a six-mile hike, one thousand feet up, and you may be cold as we climb but hot as we chug along."

Six miles of chugging? Near one of the biggest earthquake faults in the world? I was *not* looking forward to it. Even though

Barbara was also one of the Promising Students, I'd rather contemplate my bright future at the Tanger outlet mall.

"Everybody on the bus!" Mr. Rhinehart wore shorts and thick socks and heavy boots. His legs were tanned and muscled, very hikey looking. The first-aid kit he strapped to his backpack didn't make me feel any happier about hiking through desert rocks. He wasn't going to suck snake venom out of my thigh, was he? He wouldn't have to make a splint out of an old tree limb for my broken arm, would he?

"Let's sit in the front!" Barbara was excited about the adventure. Her backpack was weighted down with two fat burritos from Aquí.

Sitting next to Barbara, smelling the burritos already, I watched the other smarties board the bus. They weren't just freshmen. Which is a real clue about my school—out of four grades, only thirty kids were considered "promising." Almost all of them were too nerdy for words.

Except one. *Him.* The guy I'd seen across the quad watching me with his black eyes. My heart lurched as he got on the bus.

He wore a heavy green army surplus jacket over baggy camouflage pants. His hair was thick, tar black, and in an overgrown buzz cut. His skin was smooth milk chocolate. A silver cross dangled from his right earlobe. Everything about him was exotic, scary. He even had a black tattoo circling his upper arm. I'd seen it before when I spotted him at school hanging with his Latino homeboys.

As he passed me on the bus, I felt his stare burn through my skin. His eyes were dark caves. You couldn't look in them very long without falling in and flailing around for air.

"On the way, we're going to play Geology Jeopardy!" Mr. Rhinehart said. Barbara and I groaned, but several kids behind us clapped and squealed.

"I'll give you a geologic answer," Mr. Rhinehart continued, "and you raise your hand if you know the question. Be sure to phrase it in the form of a question."

The Guy sat in the back of the bus. I found myself wishing we'd sat in the back, too.

"It divides time into eons, eras, periods, and epochs," Mr. Rhinehart began, as the bus left dusty Barstow for our destination an hour and a half away.

"What is the geologic time scale?" someone shouted.

"Raise your hand, please. But that's correct!"

I swiveled around to see who got the answer right but ended up locking gazes with *him*. He didn't smile, didn't nod or wave. He just stared at me with his bottomless black eyes, and my whole body went numb.

"It uses decay to determine the numerical ages of rocks."

By the time we reached Pearblossom, California, and the Devil's Punchbowl Visitor's Center, I practically had a graduate degree in geology.

"What is radiometric dating?" someone in the middle of the bus shouted.

Barbara was asleep next to me. I gently tapped her shoulder.

"We're *aquí*," I said, knowing she'd wake up faster if I used the Spanish form of "here" and the name of her favorite restaurant.

"*¡¿Aquí?!*"

I was right. Barbara woke up instantly and said, "I'm starving."

"Everybody out of the bus and in a line," said Mr. Rhinehart. "Five-minute bathroom break, then we're hitting the trail."

I looked around. I didn't see anything that resembled a punchbowl, satanic or otherwise. All I saw were rocky hills and tufts of scrub. And a long, uphill trail. The Guy stepped off the bus and walked toward me. A zap of electricity suddenly shot down my arms. It seemed as though he was about to say something, but Barbara tugged my sleeve and said, "C'mon. If we don't go now, we'll have to use the devil's *toilet* bowl."

By the time Barbara and I started up the hill, The Guy was way ahead.

"Look! The devil's pebble! The devil's dead branch!"

Barbara cracked jokes the whole way. As usual, she walked superfast.

"Isn't that the devil's dirt clod?"

As I raced to keep up, the cool air and Barbara's dumb jokes lifted my spirits. I guess some emotions are like menstrual cramps. When they first appear, they make you feel like curling up in a ball. But if you gut it out, they fade enough for you to ignore them and get on with it.

"Stay on the trail, kids," Mr. Rhinehart yelled over his shoulder at us. "You don't want to disturb any snakes."

"Snakes?" I gulped, staring at the ground.

Barbara chugged on up the trail.

"Rattlesnakes?" I asked.

"And others," she shouted over her shoulder.

"Others?" I hurried to catch up.

"Copperheads, sand boas, corals, kraits, mambas, vipers, probably. That kind of thing."

Two of the other Promising Students looked like they wanted to run back to the bus. Like me, they were hoping their promise wasn't about to end in a place where the devil served punch.

"Don't worry," Barbara said, panting, "Snakes are more afraid of you than you are of them."

"Chickens."

I jerked my head up. The Guy stood a few feet ahead, standing on a small boulder jutting out from the side of the trail. He said, "Snakes prefer chickens over humans."

Barbara groaned. "Yeah, like there are chickens roaming free all over Pearblossom."

He didn't blink. He just stared down at me and said, "Or rats, rabbits, mice, prairie dogs—anything they can eat in one gulp."

Jumping down from the boulder, he stood so close to me I could smell his skin. It not only looked like milk chocolate, it smelled like it, too.

"Unless it's a python," he said, not moving one inch away from me. "They can swallow a deer . . . or you. If you see a python, run."

"There aren't any pythons around here, Warren," Barbara said, exasperated. "Are you going to get out of her way or what?"

"Or what," said Warren, flashing his black eyes at me.

My heart thumped so hard I was sure it would hammer his chest. Barbara *knew* him?

"Who's your friend?" Warren asked Barbara without taking his eyes off me.

"She's not a mute," Barbara scoffed. "Ask her yourself."

A jolt of electricity now shot through my entire body. I could feel the hairs on my arms stand up. I thought my heart would leap out of my chest and bounce down the trail.

"Who are you?" he asked me, grinning.

"Libby," I squeaked, suddenly aware that the trail was on a cliff. Just then, in a flash, I realized how far I could fall if I let myself.

"Hello, Libby. I'm Warren Villegranja. My friends call me Warrenville."

part three
warrenville

chapter twenty-four

I couldn't sleep. My bedroom window was wide open; the cool night desert air chilled the room, made me snuggle beneath my blankets. Juan Dog softly snored at my feet. The whole trailer park was asleep. But I just stared out the window, at the blue sliver of moon, and thought about *him*.

"Pocahontas," Warrenville had said to me at school, the day after our field trip, suddenly appearing behind me at my locker. "Did you read about Pocahontas yet?"

I muttered, "I don't think so."

"The movie version is full of crap."

"Oh." Not knowing what else to say, I focused on shoving books into my pack. Not that I needed them, but my hands were trembling and my knees felt like Silly Putty.

"The truth is, she was only nine years old when she was kidnapped by the Jamestown colonists. She didn't look anything like the babe Disney created."

"Uh-huh."

"And her name wasn't even Pocahontas. That was her nick-name. Like P. Diddy or something. Her real name was Matoaka."

"Uh-huh."

"Why does everyone have to *lie*? That's what I want to know."

I froze. Did he expect an answer? Had he caught me in a lie? Had he heard about my dad?

"Adults say they want you to tell the truth, but even that's a lie," he went on. "No one wants to hear what's really going through a kid's head. They would freak out. Freak *out.*" Then he asked me, "Wanna get something to eat?"

I'd never met anyone like Warrenville before. He was fifteen, a sophomore, but he seemed more like twenty. His mom was dead, he told me. His dad worked for the state, sixty miles away in San Bernardino.

"You like tacos?" he asked.

"Yeah, I like tacos."

"Follow me."

Truth be told, I would have followed Warrenville anywhere.

In silence, we crossed the iron bridge to the "bad" side of town. I figured we were going to Aquí, but Warren led me into an even smaller shack with no sign on it at all. A bell on the door announced our entrance. And old lady with kinky gray hair emerged from the back and burst into a smile the moment she saw Warren. He hugged her. They spoke Spanish. When I asked if she was his grandmother, he said, "She's everybody's grandmother."

Warren ordered goat tacos.

"Goat?" I asked.

"Trust me," he said. Then he sat down at the only table in the place. Too nervous to eat anyway, I shrugged and sat across from him.

"Let me guess," he said, narrowing his eyes at me, "you think tacos taste like the food you eat at Taco Bell."

"Well, um, yeah." I mean, it's called *Taco* Bell.

"Today, you eat a real taco."

At that moment, the gray-haired lady trudged over and set two plates in front of us. Steam rose up to kiss my face. It smelled like lamb and cilantro.

"Try one," Warren said.

I swallowed. Then I picked up the warm, soft corn tortilla, folded it over the hot meat, and took a bite. The fresh lime juice intensified the flavor of the roasted goat. The tortilla tasted like flat cornbread. It was fantastic.

Warren smiled. I smiled, too. Together, we ate six goat tacos, drank mango juice, and said almost nothing. Which, bizarrely, felt exactly right.

When I got home from school that afternoon, the refrigerator was gone; our living room looked liked a living room. Dad had left a note that read, "I'm off to find a job." Rif was in his bedroom doing homework. But all that wasn't the most extraordinary part of the day. *Barbara was with me.* I was feeling so happy about Warren, I decided to swallow my embarrassment and let Barbara see where I lived. I wanted to practice opening up instead of closing down. So I held my breath, bit the inside of my cheek, and led my friend into the asylum.

"You have a pool!" Barbara squealed, as we hopped off the bus and walked under the arch that read WELCOME TO SUNSET PARK.

Mim waved from her lounge as we walked by. "Come for a swim," she shouted.

"No, thanks," I said. Then, Barbara stunned me by asking, "Why not?"

"Yeah," Mim yelled, "why not!? You still have my suit?"

"Maybe later," I called out as I tugged on Barbara's sleeve.

"It's so clean in here," she said. "All the little front yards are so neat!"

As I pulled Barbara farther into Sunset Park, I noticed, for the first time, what she was talking about. We passed a trailer with a bonsai garden in front. A tiny bridge spanned smooth, black rocks. A white Buddha meditated beneath a miniature tree. Another trailer had a winter theme, with small white rocks as snow and a fake deer with his nose painted bright red. They were actually kind of cute. I'd passed them every day and never noticed before.

"My grandmother lives here," I said, leading Barbara into Nana's kitchen and introducing them to each other.

"Wow!" Barbara said over and over inside Nana's home. "Wow! This rocks!"

"Would you girls like a little kiwi fruit salad?" Nana asked.

"Yes! Wow!"

We ate our after-school snack, then I braced myself for the moment of truth.

"Our trailer is this way," I said, swallowing, motioning toward the back door. Barbara followed me outside.

"Trailer? No way. I've seen trailers. This is no trailer!"

"Well, technically, they call them mobile homes, but—"

"It's so cool in here!"

A blast of air-conditioning hit our faces the moment we walked through the door.

"My house is so hot, you sweat in the shower!" said Barbara. "It's like iced tea in here. Refreshing!"

Refreshing? Living in a trailer? In Barstow? With a bunch of old people?

That's when I noticed that the refrigerator was gone and Dad had acted like a normal dad by getting off the couch and looking for a job. With the huge, white elephant missing, our living room looked incredibly normal. I could hear Rif's CD player down the hall. Barbara said, "Show me your room!"

I showed her my room. It had four walls and a window and a bed that was perpetually unmade. It had a white desk and a wicker chair and a bookshelf stuffed with stuff. My closet was filled with my same old clothes, and my pajamas were hanging on a hook on the back of my door, where I'd left them that morning. Standing there, in the middle of my room, seeing it through Barbara's eyes, was a revelation. It looked oddly normal. Maybe living in a mobile retirement home wasn't so weird after all.

Refreshing!

chapter twenty-five

Nana had been planning it for weeks—all year probably—and the whole trailer park was grateful. Thanksgiving dinner in the rec room was the event of the year. Nana was in charge, everyone was invited, and each year had a different theme.

"This year, it's Chinese!" Nana announced at a meeting she held to elect the decorating committee. "Szechuan turkey!"

"We can string lanterns around the pool," Charlotte suggested.

"Or one of those paper dragons!" squealed Mim.

Frieda, a widow who lived on Heavenly Way and had a stroke the year before, shouted, "Fawaahs!" but nobody understood her because one side of her face was all droopy. Nobody but Gracie, that is.

"Fireworks," she translated.

"Fabulous!"

That year, Nana had decided to combine Thanksgiving with our trailer-warming party. Mim was asked to make sesame noodles instead of her famous baked beans; Charlotte made a cake with a layer of green tea ice cream. Everyone was excited about the big event. Everyone but me.

"Should I invite him?" I asked Barbara.

"Yes."

"Then he'll know I really like him."

"So don't invite him."

"He already told me his dad wants him to spend Thanksgiving at his aunt's house in Riverside, and he doesn't want to go. I would be doing him a favor."

"Then invite him."

"How can I invite someone I barely know to meet my whole family? And the whole trailer park!"

"Then don't invite him." Barbara groaned.

Barbara was beyond tired of talking about Warrenville. She rolled her eyes every time I mentioned his name. Barbara was spending Thanksgiving weekend with us. Her dad and stepmom were taking her step-siblings to Disney World in Florida. An experience she'd had before.

"I needed another vacation after spending my vacation with the brats," she told me. So I'd asked Mom if Barbara could spend the night in our trailer and join us for Thanksgiving dinner. She'd told me to ask Nana, who, of course, said yes. "Invite the brats, too! The more the merrier."

"I'm not going to invite him," I said to Barbara, suddenly remembering the promise I made to myself when Nadine made me feel like a loser for not having a boyfriend. "It'll be just us."

"And the whole trailer park," Barbara said.

"You're right. Should I invite him?"

She sighed. "He's pretty strange, you know," she said.

"And you're normal?" I asked.

"He doesn't even like Aquí!"

"I know. But I like him. What can I say?"

What could I say? The *click* I heard in my brain was loud and distinct. Warren and I *fit* together. I just knew it. We were both outsiders. It felt right being on the outside with him.

A few days ago, at school, Warren appeared behind me and asked, "Ever sing a polyphonic secular song?"

"Huh?" I said.

"You should, because you're a Madrigal."

Another time, he cupped his hands over my eyes, the way Greg Minsky used to do, and stood there behind me, silent, until I said, "I know it's you, Warren." I always knew when Warren was near me. His whole being radiated heat. Unlike Greg Minsky, I didn't care if Warrenville stood so close to me I could feel the muscles in his body.

Since I met Warrenville, everything looked different. Desert sunsets were the most spectacular things I'd ever seen. Purple wild heliotropes were awesome. Sand swirls and scrub and tacos and centipedes were incredibly beautiful. Even watching Dirk watch the TV was wonderful because of the angelic look on his face. Seeing my mom all flushed from a great day at Wal-Mart filled me with joy. Nana's fingers, covered in wonton dough, were suddenly rays of sunlight that made me happy just looking at them.

Was it the beginning of love? I didn't know. Was he the guy I wanted to seriously kiss? Definitely.

"I should invite him," I said. "Unless you think I shouldn't."

Barbara groaned even louder and walked away.

Mr. Belfore wore a satin robe as a kimono and sweat socks with his thongs. He lived on Nirvana Street and was considered eccentric by everyone at Sunset Park. Which was saying a lot, considering Nana's toilet armoire and the tiki hut Charlotte wore as a hat. Mr. Belfore arrived at Thanksgiving dinner with a chopstick behind each ear.

"I wanted to wear them in my hair," he explained, "but I don't have any hair."

Barbara found an old Chairman Mao-type jacket in a thrift store on Main Street, and wore navy blue pants with black canvas Chinese shoes. Mim carried a Chinese fan. Unable to find anything better, I wore a long black skirt and a red satin shirt. To complete the look, I painted my fingernails in Mom's Vroooom! red nail polish, and had her buy me the reddest lipstick Wal-Mart had. Honestly, I didn't look bad.

Amazingly, even my mom and dad got into the Thanksgiving spirit. Dad bought a box of fortune cookies and handed them out to everyone; Mom made a small purse out of an empty Chinese take-out carton with glued-on sequins and everything. My parents actually seemed happy. Dad, after a month of TV Zombie Detox, was slowly coming back to life. After the long holiday weekend, he had a job interview at a car dealership in San Bernardino. Mom, tired of having aching feet, bought larger, more comfortable shoes, and joined Weight Watchers.

"I lost two and a quarter pounds!" she said at breakfast. "Only twenty more to go!"

I waited for Dad to say, "Twenty? Don't you mean fifty?" But he just grinned and said, "Way to go, Dot."

Rif and I looked at each other like our parents were aliens. Dirk burst into tears and said, "I feel so glad!"

After breakfast, Barbara came over and we helped Nana stuff the Szechuan turkey with water chestnut and peanut stuffing. Later, we filled the pool with small, flickering, floating lanterns. Mim wanted to buy carp to swim in the pool but Gracie told her they'd die in the chlorine. Incredibly, Mom found battery-operated fish in the toy department at work. They "swam" around the pool, and everything.

Mr. Belfore helped us arrange rectangular tables all around the edges of the pool, so everybody was facing one another with the twinkling water in the center. When it was all set up, Frieda said, "It's *bufa*!"

Nobody needed Gracie's translation to know what she said. "It certainly is beautiful, Frieda," Mim said.

While Barbara checked on Nana's ginger-spiced yams, I slipped into our trailer to make a phone call.

"Nadine?"

"Libby! Happy Thanksgiving!"

"You, too. That's why I'm calling."

"How are you?" she asked.

"I'm good. We're about to have dinner down by the pool. Everyone will be there soon. You?"

"Curtis is coming over. My family is here."

"Have you—?"

"Not yet. Have you?"

"No." We both knew what we were talking about. A serious kiss.

Nadine said, "I'm hoping mine will happen tonight."

"I hope so, too. For you."

"Thanks."

Neither one of us said anything for a few long seconds. We used to wrap ourselves in each other's silences like old flannel blankets. They were comfortable, familiar. Now, our silences were awkward, filled with stuff no one wanted to say.

"So—"

"So, say hi to your family for me."

"You, too."

"Okay, then."

"Okay."

She sounded relieved. I felt sad. I knew my friendship with Nadine was over. Well, not *over*, just never the same again. A month earlier, I would have thought it was impossible. But there it was—in less than three weeks, we both had begun to move on.

"Listen up, everyone!" Nana stood near the diving board, a large glass bowl in her hands. "For those who are new, we welcome you."

The gray-haired crowd and their families burst into applause. My parents grinned. Mom adjusted her sparkly purse on her arm. Mr. Belfore tapped his chopstick against his wineglass.

Nana continued. "We have a Thanksgiving tradition here at Sunset Park. Gratitude Prayers. There's a piece of paper and a pen next to each plate. Your fee for the feast we are about to partake of is to write down one thing for which you are grateful. Something in the past year."

"And if it was the worst year of your life?" someone joked.

"Even in the worst of times, there's always something to be thankful for."

I was beginning to see that she just might be right.

"I'm going to pass this bowl around the tables. Put your Gratitude Prayer in the bowl, and we'll complete the ceremony as soon as everyone is done."

Rif scoffed. "How long is this going to take? I'm starving."

I shrugged, reached for my pen. All I could think of writing was Warren, Warren, Warren, over and over. I was so grateful that Warrenville had entered my life. Even though I'd decided not to invite him, out of respect for Barbara, he was on my mind and in my heart all day.

"What did you write?" Barbara asked me after I dropped my Gratitude Prayer in the bowl and passed it on.

"Something," I said, smiling. Then I added, "I'm glad it's just you and me tonight." Without Barbara, I would have had no one.

The sun was beginning to turn the sky orange as Nana took the bowl of Gratitude Prayers to the barbecue she'd set up in the corner. Small flames flickered above the rim. She set the bowl down, plunged one hand into the sea of papers, and began to read aloud.

"I'm thankful for another year of life."

"For the raise in Social Security."

"AARP discounts."

After she read each one, she tossed it into the fire and we watched it sizzle up to heaven.

"Lipitor."

"Fosamax."

"Viagra."

Everyone twittered at the litany of prescription drugs. Nana continued reading.

"I'm thankful for my parents' health."

"For a roof over our heads . . . even though it's a metal roof." The group laughed again. Nana looked at Mom and smiled.

"For new friends." Barbara looked at me and grinned.

"Dark sunglasses." (Rif's, of course.)

"Roasted sesame oil." Everyone knew that was Nana's. "And family dinners."

"Orthopedic shoes."

"Grandchildren."

"Sundays."

"For learning how to let go."

Yeah, that was mine. It was embarrassing to hear it out loud. Still, I was glad I wrote it. Even though I wasn't sure I knew how it felt to let it *all* go, I was incredibly grateful that I was starting to learn. A month ago, my life was over. Now, it felt as though a new life was beginning. I felt sad for losing what I had, but— amazingly—I was feeling excited about the future. It's weird how everything can suddenly look up when your whole world is down the drain.

Nana kept reading the Gratitude Prayers.

"Laser eye surgery."

"Plastic surgery."

The group snickered again. Nana finally burned the last of the prayers. She held her hands together, tilted her head back, and said, "God, please accept our thanks. We all hope to talk to you at our dinner next year." Then she hollered, "Let's eat!"

With that, several of the older grandchildren paraded in with plates of steaming food. The air smelled of ginger and scallions. Juan yipped under the table. Nana passed me and kissed the top of my head.

"Goat tacos!"

A familiar voice bellowed from outside the pool's gate.

Yip. Yip.

The group stopped passing food and stared. My heart fluttered.

"I'm grateful for goat tacos and chipotle chilis."

Warren opened the gate and walked in.

I stood up. "What are you—? How did you—?"

The group resumed chattering, reaching, scooping, and eating. I heard Mr. Belfore say, "I'm grateful for this pork bao."

"Barbara invited me," Warren said, as she scooted over to make room for him.

I gaped at her. She quietly asked, "A person can have a boyfriend *and* a best friend, can't she?"

Best friend? Boyfriend? I was too happy to let either label weird me out. Not that night, when everything felt so right. Flinging my arms around Barbara, I couldn't stop grinning. Nana walked up to us.

"Sorry I'm late," said Warren, extending his hand shyly. "I'm Libby's friend, Warren Villegranja."

Nana shook his hand warmly. "Anyone who's thankful for goat tacos and chipotle chilis will always be welcome in my home."

chapter twenty-six

I suspected that somewhere, out there, there were Thanksgiving dinners like this. We laughed, savored the food, and enjoyed one another's company without tension as thick as lumpy gravy.

Mom was on the other side of the pool, and Dad had wandered off somewhere. Rif nodded his head, saying hi. He'd seen Warrenville at school. Dirk giggled and blushed.

"Scallion pancake?" Barbara asked Warren.

"Why not?"

I started to explain my nutty grandmother and her traditions, but Warren didn't seem to care. He piled his plate high and ate heartily. He reached under the table and squeezed my knee. My whole insides were flooded with light. I felt warm and astonishingly calm. Warren fit in so easily and naturally, I forgot to be ashamed of the trailer park and my elderly neighbors. I even hugged Mim and let Juan nestle into her chins. I ate seconds of everything without once worrying that my satin shirt might pull at its Chinese buttons. Thanksgiving came only once a year, after all.

As candles flickered atop the pool, paper lanterns swayed in the desert breeze, and garlic and ginger infused the air, I felt happier than I'd ever felt in my life. It wasn't Warren or Barbara or Thanksgiving. It was more than that. Suddenly, without warning bells or bugles trumpeting, I felt totally, completely, absolutely *normal.*

"Elizabeth Madrigal?"

A man in a policeman's uniform stood behind me. Instantly, I panicked. I flashed back to Chatsworth and Rif's arrest and bill collectors at the door.

"Yes?" I said, weakly, "I'm Elizabeth Madrigal."

He looked confused, said, "Is there another Elizabeth Madrigal? An older lady?"

"Oh! Yes! My grandmother." Heart pounding, I stood up and led the officer around the pool to Nana. Her face darkened as he got closer.

"What happened?" she asked abruptly.

Quietly, he answered, "There's been an accident. Your son. He's okay, but he's in the hospital."

"My son?"

Nana and I both spun around to look for my dad. Mom sat alone by the diving board next to Frieda. Another surge of panic rushed through my body. Where was my father?

"He must be in the bathroom," I blurted out.

The police officer placed his hand gently on my shoulder. "I'm sorry," he said.

Nana swung into action. "Libby, get your mom and your

brothers and meet me at the gate."

In a daze, I did what I was told. I never said a word to Barbara or Warren, just followed my family to the front gate of Sunset Park where we silently waited for a taxi. Our old Toyota, the only car our family had, was gone.

Nobody could speak. We were too stunned, too hurt, to form any words at all.

"I didn't want anyone smelling beer on my breath," Dad explained drunkenly, from his bed at Barstow General. "I was going to order extra onions."

My father had left Thanksgiving dinner to drive to the only open liquor store in town and buy a case of beer. He'd sat there, in the liquor store parking lot, chugging one can after the other. Then, to cover his tracks, he'd headed for the landmark McDonald's to order a burger, extra onions. Only he was too drunk to drive. My father's right fender rammed the corner of McDonald's converted railroad car, knocking it off its foundation. Thankfully, McDonald's was closed for the holiday. No one was hurt but my father. Dad broke his nose. The fire chief told us they found him passed out at the wheel.

"Why, Lot?" Mom asked him in the hospital. "Why?"

It was a question we all wanted answered. He'd been doing so well! But Dad didn't say anything. He hung his head and sat there, like a zombie, his glasses falling off his bandaged nose. I couldn't look at him anymore. I felt so disappointed I wanted to bury my head in a pillow and sob.

So much for gratitude.

So much for beginning to feel normal.

chapter twenty-seven

Dad's accident made the local news that night and the front page of the paper the next morning. The newspaper photograph was too mortifying for words. My father was handcuffed and dazed, his nose bloody. Two uniformed police officers stood on either side of him. The caption read:

FRIES WITH THAT?
**Drunk Barstow Man Slams into
Landmark McDonald's Restaurant**

My dad: Drunk Barstow Man. I felt like someone had let all the air out of my life. I felt flat, deflated. And the worst part of all? I didn't hear a word from Warrenville. Not one word over the entire Thanksgiving break.

* * *

If you ask me, we *all* got busted. Mom made us stand behind Dad, as a family, in front of the Barstow judge. His gavel hit the wood with a loud *clack*.

"Your driver's license is suspended for six months," he said. "You'll pay restitution to McDonald's, perform one hundred and eighty hours of community service, and go straight into the rehab center."

Mom raised her hand.

"Yes?" the judge asked, looking annoyed.

"I was wondering, your honor, if you could order the whole family into counseling?"

Rif gasped. I stamped my foot and Dirk started to cry. Nana, standing erect and proud next to us added, "I'll second that motion."

The judge rolled his eyes. "I can't force your whole family into anything, Mrs. Madrigal. But I will strongly suggest it to your husband's rehab counselor."

Rif exploded. "Mistrial!"

The judge narrowed his eyes at Rif and asked, "Are you Richard Madrigal?"

Rif swallowed. Dad said, "Yes, your honor, he's my son."

Peering through half-frame glasses, the judge flipped through a folder on his desk. "Have you completed *your* community service?" he asked Rif.

Rif stared straight ahead, speechless.

The judge said, "The computer spit out your name. Just because you move doesn't mean you're free from paying your debt to society."

"I didn't mean it about a mistrial. Really, sir." Rif blinked and tried to look innocent.

"Richard, your community service starts this weekend. You'll remove the graffiti from the boulders in the Mojave River bed. That is an order."

Big and Little Moe? I wondered. The judge added, "You'll be given the supplies. Be sure to wear sunscreen."

"But—" Rif started.

"Next case." The judge's gavel came down hard.

On the way home, Mom came down hard, too. "This family is going to pull itself together if it kills us." Then she asked, "Who's hungry for a low-cal *snackywacky*?"

chapter twenty-eight

There we were. All of us. In *therapy*. Ugh. Dad's rehab was in Victorville, so the rest of us drove down there for family sessions with him.

"Why are you here?" the therapist asked us in the first session. His name was Josh, and since he didn't ask us to call him Dr. Josh, I assumed he never quite made it to med school.

Josh went around the circle. "Rif? Why are you here?"

"It's a family outing," he said sarcastically.

"Lot?"

"The court made me."

"Libby?"

"My mother made me."

"Dirk?"

"I dunno."

"Elizabeth?"

"I'm here for my son."

"Dot?"

"I don't know what else to do."

Josh–Just–Josh nodded his head. "Is anyone here because they need help?"

We sat stiff and silent, like six trees in the Madrigal petrified forest.

"Okay," Josh said, adjusting his frameless glasses with his slender, girly fingers. "Over the next few weeks, you may feel different about why you're here. In this group, we'll cry, yell, laugh, feel awful, feel great, feel awful again. You name it, we're going there. The point is to fully explore what it means to grow up in an alcoholic family, what it means to be an alcoholic, what happens to the spouse of an alcoholic, and how some kids act out and act *up* under the stress of it all."

"I'm not an alcoholic," Dad mumbled.

Rif and I side-glanced at each other.

"That's the perfect place to begin," Josh said. "*Definitions.* Everybody ready to dive in?"

Nobody said a word. So our skinny therapist, with his bushy brown hair and wrinkly white shirt, who looked like he was still in high school, dove in by himself.

"Alcoholism is a chronic disease that often gets worse over time and can kill you if not treated."

Dad sighed. Nana nodded. Mom fished around in her purse for a Kleenex.

The only window in the therapy room was covered in vertical Levolor blinds. Not that there was anything to look at. But staring at a dreary parking lot was better than sitting in a circle and "sharing my feelings" with Just Josh and my family.

"Basically, if using alcohol is causing *any* continuous disruption in an individual's personal, social, spiritual, or economic life—and the individual doesn't stop using alcohol—that would be *harmful* dependence. Often, denial and rationalization become a way of life. Does any of this sound familiar?"

Mom looked at her hands. Dad said, "I'm not in denial. I'm just not an alcoholic."

Rif laughed out loud. Dad shot him a look.

Josh asked, "Rif, do you have something to say?"

"Yeah," said Rif. "Three words: Barstow trailer park."

The rest of us stopped breathing. No one had ever stood up to my father like that. In *public*, too. I looked at the window again. If it was open, I would have leaped out.

"What do you mean by that?" Josh asked.

Boldly, Rif looked directly at Dad. "If you're not an alcoholic, Dad, why did you lose your job and our house? Why did we have to move into a trailer bought by your mother?"

"Yes, Lot," Mom piped up. "Why?"

Now I considered jumping through the glass. Anything to get out of that room. Dad apparently had the same idea. He got red in the face. His nostrils flared when he stood up and said, "I don't have to put up with this crap." Kicking his chair, Dad headed for the door.

"Actually, Mr. Madrigal," Josh said, "you do. This is part of your court-mandated rehab."

Dad stopped. But he didn't sit down.

Josh added softly, "Would you rather go to jail?"

His question hung in the air. The tension in the room felt like a saddle on my back. Suddenly I wanted to scream and pound the walls with my fists. I wanted to rip the scarlet letter off my chest, stop being the daughter of the "Drunk Barstow Man." I wanted *answers*! Why did Dad start drinking after he stopped? How could Nadine move on so fast? Why won't Warren call me or even look at me at school? When I saw him on campus, I swear he saw me, but he looked away fast and stayed in the tight circle of his friends. Why did everything always go wrong at the precise moment it seemed like it might—for once—go right?

Barbara had said, "Boys are jerks." But I knew that wasn't true. Not Warren. It was me. Something was wrong with *me*.

"Please take a seat, Mr. Madrigal," Josh said.

Dad sat. He crossed his arms in front of his chest and slouched so low in the chair he nearly disappeared.

For a few long moments, Josh didn't say anything. Nobody said anything. It was the loudest silence I've ever heard. Finally, Josh cleared his throat and looked each of us in the eye.

"I'd like to try something a little unconventional. Is everyone up for it?"

Still, nobody said a word.

"Here's what I'd like you to do," he said. "For our next session, I'd like each of you to write a letter to Lot about how his drinking has affected you personally. The letters should be specific and completely honest. Spill your guts. Tell him how you really feel. We'll read them at the next session. Are you all willing?"

Mom nodded her head energetically. The rest of us shrugged.

Dad asked, "What am I supposed to do?"

Josh answered, "Listen."

chapter twenty-nine

Writing my dad that letter was one of the hardest things I've ever done. I held a pen in my hand for almost an hour before the words began to flow. After not saying stuff for so many years, it felt like I was stabbing him in the back. I mean my *dad*. How could I tell him the honest-to-God truth?

But I did. I spilled my guts in a letter. Next, I needed to find the guts to read it out loud to him.

Nana drove us to Victorville the following week. On the way, my family talked about school, sand, Thai food, carbs—anything but the letters we all carried. I was a basket case. Would my father hate me after I read him my letter? Would he refuse to come home? Was this the beginning of the end of my family?

Josh greeted us all with handshakes. Dad was already in the therapy room. He kissed Mom, hugged his mother and us. He seemed relaxed. Which made me feel even worse. How could I hurt him when he'd been living next door in the rehab center working hard on getting better?

"Let's get started," Josh said. We all sat down and he said, "First, I want to acknowledge how hard it was for everyone to write their letters. I also want to recognize how difficult it will be for Lot to hear what his family has to say. But you have to feel the hurt before you can heal. And healing is what we're all about here. Who wants to read his or her letter first?"

Dirk raised his hand.

"Go ahead, Dirk," Josh said.

Dirk opened his letter and burst into tears.

"It's okay to cry," Josh said, softly. "It's okay to feel whatever you feel."

Is it okay to feel like leaping through the window? I wondered, my pulse racing.

Sniffing, Dirk read his letter.

"Dear Daddy,

"When you get drunk, you make me scared. You yell at Mom and Juan, and sometimes me. It makes me want to cry. And once, I saw Mom crying in the laundry room, when she didn't know I saw her. But I knew she was crying because of you. Please stop drinking.

"Love, Dirk."

Dirk sniffed again, and wiped his nose on his sleeve.

"Very good, Dirk, thank you," said Josh. Dad started to speak, but Josh held up his hand and said, "I'd like you to wait until all the letters are read before you comment. Would you be willing to do that?"

Dad nodded.

"Good. Rif? Would you like to go next?"

"Our dog ate my letter," Rif said, smirking.

Josh didn't react. Instead, he turned to me and said, "Libby? Ready?"

Instantly, my heart pumped blood into my ears. My palms got sweaty and I felt light-headed.

Josh said, "It's okay. Take a deep breath."

I took a deep breath, shakily opened my letter, stared at it, and read.

"Dear Dad:

"My heart is pounding as I write this letter. Now that it's finally time to tell you how I feel, I'm nervous. I don't want you to hate me. But I do want you to know how it feels to be the daughter of a dad who disappears little by little every day, right before my eyes. It's scary. One day, will you be gone forever? I miss the funny, smart dad I used to have. Drunk Dad is mean. He's embarrassing. He makes me mad. It's like you'd rather ruin our lives than stop drinking, which seems really selfish. And you've made me feel ashamed of you, when I used to think I had the coolest dad in the world. How could you do that?

"Remember that camping trip we took to Big Bear Lake?

*You and Mom rented an RV. Rif and I played crazy
eights in the back. Dirk was just a baby, so he slept the
whole way. I keep thinking about that first night, around
the fire pit, eating s'mores and making up ghost stories. It
was all of us. Together. It wasn't anything special, but I
think, maybe, it was the happiest night of my life.
Because our family was just like every other family. We
were normal.*

*"I don't know if I can explain this right, but your drinking
makes me feel empty. In the same way that night at Big
Bear Lake made me feel full. Your drinking makes me feel
lost, like I don't belong anywhere.*

*"Mostly, Dad, I feel like something is wrong with me.
Something is missing. I don't know what it is, or if I can
blame you for me feeling so . . . unnormal. Maybe this is
what kids feel like when their parent dies. Because, it's
kind of like you did die. The real you. The Dad who's
only in my memory now.*

"Love, Libby."

Too scared to look up, I didn't. I waited for Josh to say something,
but he didn't, either. Instead, Dad's voice was the first sound I
heard.

"I'm so sorry, baby," he said, almost whispering. Josh didn't
cut him off. "You're right. I have been selfish. I'm so, so sorry."

"Thank you, Libby," Josh said. "And you, Lot. We have a long
way to go, but we've taken a huge first step."

Mom and Nana went after me. They both cried all the way through their letters, both said how hard it was to see Dad destroy himself. But I could barely hear them through the loud thumping of my heart.

chapter thirty

Barbara's stepmother decorated their whole house with stuffed animals. I swear, there were fake furry things in every room. Except Barbara's.

"She knows better than to set foot in here," Barbara said. A sign on her purple-painted bedroom door read BEWARE: HAZARDOUS MATERIALS INSIDE. I think it was actually true. I found an Oreo under her bed with green hair growing on it.

Since I'd begun family counseling, Barbara was full of questions.

"Have you cried yet?

"Has your dad cried?

"Is Just Josh anything like Dr. Phil?"

Me, I just had one question: "Why is Warren avoiding me?"

Barbara groaned. "Who knows?"

"Why do you *think*?"

"Why don't you ask him?"

"Yeah, like I'm going to ask him why he dumped me when we weren't even together!"

Barbara sighed. "Want a Fudgsicle?"

"No."

At that moment, I made a decision. Josh had explained that an alcoholic's family members often "walk on eggshells" around the user, trying not to rock the boat. They stuff their own feelings and feel isolated because they don't want to face what's really going on. I'd done that hundreds of times before. But no more.

Standing up, I marched to Barbara's bedroom door.

"I want answers. Are you with me?"

"Where are we going?" Barbara asked, excited.

"You'll see. Follow me."

We marched across the old iron bridge, over broken beer bottles, past Aquí, almost to the base of the Calico Mountains. We walked and walked and walked. Since it was December, it was warm instead of hot. But the wind whipped sand into our faces and up our noses. By the time we got where we were going, my green canvas shoes were white with dust and my lungs were full of dirt.

"The old drive-in?" Barbara asked.

"Rif told me this is where all the guys hang out."

Barstow's Skyview Drive-In was a huge, empty dirt lot, surrounded by a chain-link fence. The large movie screen was still there, as was the old Snack Shack, but all the speakers were gone. Clearly, no one had seen a movie there in years. Barbara and I snuck through a hole in the fence. The noise was deafening. I could hear engines revving and guys yelling, "I'm next!" A thick dust cloud swallowed up the action in the middle of the lot. As soon as it cleared, I saw Rif.

"His time is up!" he shouted. "I'm next!"

Barbara and I hung back and watched my brother hand some guy five dollars, and hop on a dune buggy. He gunned the engine, then hurtled forward yelping, "Wahoo!"

It looked incredibly dangerous and incredibly fun. Rif rode the dune buggy in a circle, like it was a bucking bronco. The wheels kicked up so much dust it was hard to see anything. Was this even legal? Probably not, since the only adult there was the guy taking all the kids' cash.

"A buck a minute," the cash guy yelled. "Two-minute minimum."

After five minutes, a bullhorn blared and Rif slowed down. As the dust fell back to the earth, I scanned the crowd. It didn't take long to see him. His black hair was gray with dirt, and his brown skin was ashen. Still, my heart lurched. I tried to will his dark eyes to turn and look at me, but Warrenville was in line to ride the dune buggy next. He forked over five bucks and hopped on as soon as Rif hopped off.

Instead of riding in a circle, Warren revved the engine and drove straight for the far fence. I panicked. It looked as though he'd ram right into it. But he swerved just in time and careened over a huge dirt pile, flying through the air and landing on all four wheels. The crowd went wild.

"Did you see that?" I asked Barbara, excited.

She scoffed. "Macho man."

As soon as the dust settled, Warrenville and I locked gazes. In the middle of shaking the dirt out of his hair, he caught sight of me, and my heart kicked up its disco beat. Barbara and I were the only girls at the drive-in. In fact, I heard someone ask, "Who let *them* in?"

But I didn't care. I was there for one reason and one reason alone.

"Can I talk to you for a second?" I said, walking straight up to Warren even though my legs wobbled like rubber bands. Barbara waited for me near the Snack Shack.

"Oooo. Warrenville gets busted!"

"Mommy wants you home."

The boys in line made fun, but I didn't care. "It'll only take a second," I said.

Warren nodded. He led me over to the far fence, away from the action, and said, "Yeah?"

There he was, inches from my face, his caterpillar eyebrows up, waiting. My heart hammered my rib cage. My tongue felt like a piece of cardboard.

"You know that Santa-Claus-down-the-chimney thing?" I said. "It's a *crock*. Totally made up! A fat guy could never slide down a chimney. Why do people lie? That's what I want to know."

Warren smiled softly. He remembered his rant about Pocahontas.

"I was wondering," I said, biting my lower lip, "is everything okay? I haven't seen you much at school."

Warren stopped smiling, looked away. "Yeah," he said. "Everything's fine. I've been around."

I waited for him to say something more, but the next thing he said felt like an ice pick to the chest.

229

"I've gotta go. My friends are waiting."

Warren sauntered away and I nearly crumpled to the dusty ground. If Barbara hadn't appeared, I probably would have stayed there, in a heap, until the dry wind blew me away.

That night, as I was getting ready for bed, our phone rang. I got it by the third ring.

"Hello?"

"I did it," Nadine squealed.

"Did what?"

"Had a serious kiss!"

Oh.

How could I tell the girl I used to tell *everything* to that I didn't want to hear about the happiest moment in her life? How could I tell her I was feeling too upset and confused to even care? When I'd gotten home, I'd taken a shower, washed the dirt from Skyview Drive-In down the drain. I couldn't wait to crawl under the covers and pull a blanket over my life.

"Great! What was it like?" I asked, forcing my voice to sound cheery.

"Awesome! Incredible! It was everything we imagined it would be that day in your backyard. My knees got weak and my heart pounded and I thought fireworks would shoot off the top of my head. Curtis is a *great* kisser. Very dramatic. He sort of bent me over backward like we were in an old movie or something. Kissing him felt like the whole world was on fire!"

"Wow." It's all I could think of to say. Then I added, "I'm really happy for you, Nadine." And I was. At least one of us would know love.

"You'll get your kiss, too," she said. "One day. You'll see."

In my head, I figured she was probably right. But in my heart, a serious kiss—true love—felt as far away as the distant look in Warrenville's eyes.

chapter thirty-one

By mid-December, Barstow store owners had trotted out their tired holiday decorations and the weather cooled to a comfy sixty degrees. Each day, I got up, got dressed, caught the bus, and went to school. When we weren't at Aquí, Barbara and I hung out at her place or mine. Rif scrubbed graffiti off Big and Little Moe, Mom had manicures during her lunch breaks at Wal-Mart, Dad got better in Victorville, Dirk played video games, and Nana made Ethiopian food with chickpeas.

"Not many people know that the Ethiopian Christmas holiday is celebrated on January seventh," she said. "Part of the traditional holiday meal is a sourdough pancake called *injera* that acts as an edible plate!"

Things were back to normal at the Madrigal mobile homes — well, as normal as life can get when your dad is in rehab and the boy you thought was "the one" barely nods his head when he sees you at school.

"Guys are jerks," Barbara said again. But it didn't make me feel any better.

The one bright spot in that dismal month was—believe it or not—our therapy sessions with Just Josh and Dad. I learned a lot.

"An alcoholic parent is like having a 'king baby' in the family," Josh said during one session. "Instead of being mature and responsible and taking care of the kids, like a well-functioning parent does, the king baby is grown but still immature. He requires a lot of attention, the way babies do. In fact, he becomes the center of attention. The whole family is always watching him, watching out for him, covering for him."

Mom leaned forward, listening intently.

"When there's a king baby in a family," Josh continued, "the children are forced to grow up before they are really ready to. They have to parent the king baby in a sense, because he's not up to the job of parenting them. It's very scary for kids. It feels unsafe, which creates a tremendous amount of anxiety. Because, you see, the child knows deep down that he or she is really faking it, *pretending* to be able to handle it all. But, of course, she can't, can she? After all, she's just a kid. Does this sound familiar?"

"Yes!" Rif and I said in unison. Dirk look scared.

Another time, Josh explained how family members can become so entangled in the life of the alcoholic, they forget to have a life of their own.

"It's important to detach, with love. No one is responsible for Lot's behavior but Lot himself. You all have to let go."

Nana nodded and smiled at me.

Maybe because we were all there ready to listen, or maybe because he was ready to talk, my father slowly began to open up.

"Just like you, Libby," he said, barely above a whisper, "I watched my father disappear. He sold insurance in San Bernardino. We had a house, a normal life, the three of us. Until his drinking took over. Just before I graduated high school, we lost the house. My parents moved to Nana's trailer in Barstow. It wasn't a nice retirement home then, it was a dump. I lived with my friend's family in San Bernardino until I graduated. I was so ashamed of my dad, I told everyone he got a job as a dealer in Vegas."

Glancing around the room, I noticed my brothers looked the same way I did—*agog*. We'd never heard any of this before. The mere mention of my grandfather was taboo in our house. *Shhh! Don't tell.* For the first time in my fourteen years, I understood why.

"My father was the man I most wanted *not* to be," Dad said, "and here I am, exactly like him."

Josh said, "That's why we're here. To break the pattern."

After that session, Dad took Mom's hand and led her into the hallway outside the therapy room. My brothers and I followed until Nana said, "Let's give them a few minutes alone, okay?"

We nodded and hung back. Still, I could hear my dad ask my mom, "Why have you and the kids stuck by me all these years?"

Mom didn't hesitate. "Because we're a family," she said. "And that's what families do."

At that moment—for the first time since I can remember—I felt like I really did belong in my family. We belonged together. For better or worse.

On the last day before Christmas vacation, I felt a hand tap my shoulder as I organized my locker.

"Hang on, Barbara," I said, without turning around. "I'm almost done."

"Libby."

The voice was male, familiar. I wheeled around, and there he was.

"Hey," Warren said.

I just stared at him, my heart thudding, unable to think of a word to say.

"I've been a jerk," he said.

Even more speechless, my mouth hung open.

"Can you come with me?" he asked. "I want to show you something."

I nodded. Truth was, after everything, I'd still follow Warrenville anywhere.

We left campus, walked down the hill, and continued across the iron bridge.

"Insects breathe through tiny pores in their bellies," Warren mentioned, as we crossed the dry riverbed. "And dragonflies have the best eyesight of almost all insects."

I grinned. Warren was always full of so many obscure facts.

"Did you know that the average male has up to twenty-five thousand hairs on his face?"

"No, I didn't know that."

"Now you do," he said, grinning back at me.

Eventually, my heart stopped racing, and a blanket of calm engulfed me. Maybe I'd been through too much to feel tense anymore, or maybe it was something else. Something about

Warrenville that relaxed me. I let him take me where he wanted me to go. I let life flow.

We turned left after Big Moe and walked up a dusty road. There weren't many houses around, just dried fields and scrub. Until we came to clearing. A small, metal arch marked the entrance to a cemetery. The wrought-iron gate was open. It was tiny, nothing like Oakwood Cemetery in Chatsworth, and old. Some of the gravestones were so wind whipped you couldn't read who was buried there. Others were brand-new. Warren took my hand. A surge of electricity shot through my whole arm.

He said, "I want you to meet my mom."

Warren led me to a small headstone at the far end of the cemetery. It read HERE LIES CECILIA VILLEGRANJA, BELOVED WIFE AND MOTHER.

Squeezing my hand, Warren said, "My mother was killed by a drunk driver. Right out there." He pointed up the road.

I looked up the dusty, deserted road. When I turned back, Warren was facing me.

"I freaked out about your dad. I'm sorry. I know it's not your fault. I'm pissed at all drunk drivers. How could someone drive when he's high? When someone's mom could be on the road walking home from work? How could anyone do that?"

"I don't know," I said, quietly.

"I shouldn't have cut you out. I'm sorry. I went a little crazy."

"It's okay, Warren. I went a little crazy, too."

Bending down to shake the dust off the dried flowers decorating his mother's grave, Warren said, "Mom didn't like fresh flowers. She hated to watch things die."

chapter thirty-two

The desert behind Warrenville's house goes on forever. He lives in the middle of nowhere, beyond the outskirts of Barstow. It took us half an hour just to get there. His house was a patchwork of plaster patches and wooden supports.

"Each week something new falls apart," he said. "Each week my dad and I patch it back up. Dad calls it our quilt house."

I thought about my house in Chatsworth and our Barstow trailer, how ashamed I was of them. Now, looking at Warrenville's funky mended house, and his obvious love for it, my cheeks got hot. Why have I wasted so much time worrying about what other people think? How stupid is that?

The sun was still high in the sky as Warren and I shared a soda in his backyard.

"It's so dead around here," I said.

"Dead?"

"The desert, I mean," I added quickly.

"Girl, there's *nothing* dead about a desert." Standing, Warren took my hand and led me far into the flat, dirt-brown field beyond his house. "When I was growing up, my mother showed me all the life here. That's a heliotrope there, over there a yellow linanthus." He pointed to wildflowers popping through the dry desert soil.

"That's a brown-eyed evening primrose." He kicked a stone off into the emptiness. A low, dry bush rustled. "If we stood here silently, and didn't move until dark, we could watch the desert wake up before our eyes. Coyotes, owls, iguana, prairie dogs, jackrabbits, rattlesnakes . . ."

I winced. "Maybe we should move."

"Why?"

"I hate snakes."

"How can you hate snakes? That's like saying you hate *nature*. Without snakes, the eagle might die of starvation, the desert would be overrun with rats. Snakes are as beautiful as bats, as beautiful as scorpions, as beautiful as . . ."

He went on. I just stared at him, smiled inside. In truth, there was nothing as beautiful as he was. His cheeks were aflame in the sunlight, his black eyes even blacker and more intense against the powder blue desert sky.

". . . as beautiful as vultures and tarantulas . . ." Warren continued his list. I longed to touch his face, his hair. I wanted to reach under his jacket sleeve and trace my fingertip all the way around his tattoo.

". . . as a wild donkey," Warren went on. "As beautiful as a black widow spider, as a fish . . ."

"Hey, wait a minute," I interrupted. "There aren't any *fish* in the desert."

"That's what you think," he said. "Pupfish live in mineral hot springs throughout the desert. Like I told you, there's life and beauty everywhere. You just have to know where to look."

I knew exactly where to look. Straight into Warrenville's eyes.

"You're right," I said softly, my voice suddenly buried deep within my chest.

"I know," he said, just as softly, right back at me.

Suddenly, Warren took a step closer to me and reached for my hand. He lifted it up to his chest, held it against his beating heart. "This is *my* life," he whispered. My heart thumped, too.

I stood absolutely still. Afraid to breathe, afraid to move. The rhythm of our two hearts seemed to shake the whole earth. Suddenly, Warren's face was against my face, and his lips were against my lips. They felt velvety. He smelled like fresh cilantro; he smelled like spring. I pressed my lips harder against his and he parted his mouth, wrapped one arm around me, flattened my hand against his pounding heart. We kissed. I melted into his body. Our kiss lasted a lifetime. I could hear the flutter of desert life awakening around me. Or was it me? Was it *my* life awakening around me?

All I knew for sure was that Nadine was mistaken. It was nothing like our fantasy that day on the rafts in my Chatsworth backyard. My knees weren't buckling; I wasn't on the verge of passing out. I wasn't ready to explode. This kiss felt like cashmere. My body felt light, like it was floating. This kiss was as deep as the center of the Atlantic, as wide as the Pacific. It was shelter in a storm, a cool breeze in the desert, a bonfire in the snow. This kiss felt safe and exciting at the same time. It was hot butterscotch melting over vanilla ice cream; it was a down pillow. This kiss—at long last my serious kiss—felt like arriving, belonging, being loved, loving.

"You," Warren whispered.

He didn't say anything more. He didn't have to. He just kissed me again. And it felt like coming home. That much I'd been right about. A serious kiss feels like *home.* Pulling back the curtains and letting in the light and coming home.

It's complete. It's the beginning. It's the end of emptiness.

It's love. The big it.

It's life, in a desert, if you know where to look.